ATOM

First published in Great Britain in 2014 by Corsair

1 3 5 7 9 10 8 6 4 2

A CIP catalogue record for this book is available from the British Library.

ISBN 978-1-472110-98-5 (paperback)
ISBN 978-1-472113-57-3 (eBook)

Designed and typeset by Carrdesignstudio.com
Illustrated by Ellie Denwood

Printed and bound by CPI Group (UK) Ltd, Croydon, CR0 4YY

Papers used by Atom are from well-managed forests
and other responsible sources.

MIX
Paper from
responsible sources
FSC® C104740

Atom
An imprint of
Little, Brown Book Group
Carmelite House
50 Victoria Embankment
London EC4Y 0DZ

An Hachette UK Company
www.hachette.co.uk

www.atombooks.net

For Gran,
who would have liked this,
I think.

ONE

'Tell the story to its end,' says Eren with a grin. His yellow eyes are glowing like embers in the night.

'When I reach the end,' I say, 'what happens? You'll have the whole story.'

'Pff!' he laughs. 'Have it? Have it and own it? Boy,' he says, 'I am the whole story.'

'Then what happens if I tell you the last bit?'

'*When* you tell me, you mean. What happens then?'

I nod. He's huge. There's no attic now, no window, no lights. Just Eren. Eren, and nothing after that.

He's thinking about something and he smiles. 'Hmm,' he says, looking at me and licking his lips with a dry, grey tongue. 'What happens then? Why don't we find out?'

Somewhere in my stomach I feel cold and sad. I'm lonely, but the story goes on.

'There were things you missed,' he says. 'Eh? Weren't there? Stick with those feelings. The sadness. The hunger. The bump, bump, bump of confusions and hurtings! Oh, boy! Oh, yes. Stick with them. They're good. I like those ones. The dark ones. The real ones.

Let me hear those. Tell me 'bout that.'

I nod. 'Dark ones?'

'Tell me.' He leans forward, eager, like a child that can't hold back.

I start to talk, and I hear my voice in the blackness. What am I saying? I hear my voice. 'I remember the moon. It was bright and slim. It looked like a knife in the sky . . .'

He licks his lips and laughs and listens.

⁂

THE MOON was bright and slim as a knife, a scratch of light in the sky. It glinted off the water on the road. Clump, clump, clump. Another jolt, another bump. I reached forward to squeeze Mum's hand. 'What a ride!'

She smiled and nodded. She didn't want to talk. 'Yeah. Quite a ride. Can't be long now, though. There soon, I'm sure. There soon.'

I fogged the window with my breath. Moonlight was shining off the branches of the trees outside. Mum always hated travelling. Anything was better than this road, all rocks and grass and puddles and nothing like London. She was clinging to the seat so hard that her knuckles had turned white. The forest went on and on. It was huge, black, all pine trees and shadows stretching up from the road and rolling over the horizon, crashing into the sky.

'Not long now,' she said again.

'Not that either,' said our driver, and he slowed the car

right down. Mr Pugh smelled of smoke and sang songs while he drove, all under his breath with a grin spread wide on his face. I heard him muttering in his croaky voice, 'Easy, now! Whoa, whoa! Steady, gal,' talking to the car like it was a horse.

Weird.

I looked back out the window, searching around. The trees were clearing away and I could make out the lights of a village ahead. Ever seen the way light catches on fish when they splash and jump in water? They looked like that, the houses and everything, all sitting in the valley, shining out, blinking at the night sky.

'We're on the last stretch now, ma'am,' said Mr Pugh, 'so I'd think, eh, ten minutes, give or take. Should be less bumpy from now.'

'Thank you, Mr Pugh,' said Mum, and she sighed with relief. Her cheeks were flushing red. She turned in her seat to face me, smiled again and winked. 'Soon there, he said! Better get your scarf on, Oli, it's a cold night. Can you believe it's July? If it gets much worse it'll kill the poor flowers.'

I pressed my nose against the glass. I made myself not think of London, not think of everything I'd miss. I stared into the night, just stared and stared and waited. I could feel every flinch of Mum's hands.

'There's, like, no buildings,' I said.

'Ha! No *tall* buildings, perhaps. You're spoiled in the city, Oli. Coxborough is big enough. And you get to meet Rob at last. And see how the house looks.'

My Uncle Rob and his tiny country town. I'd never been

here, never met him before, never even heard his voice on the phone, but suddenly here we were, on the way to my grandmother's house. *Our new home*, Mum had said. *For now.* I'd heard about the fun she'd had there growing up, about the games and the food and the light, and then about Gran's sickness, and the quiet and the dust and the sadness. It'd been empty for years, but Uncle Rob had moved back in, to build a life and make things better.

'Ah, it's been too long! I really wish we'd brought you out here before. If only your father would just—' She stopped and tutted and looked away.

'When's Dad coming?'

Mum sucked in her breath and sat up. 'Soon! Honestly, where's your spirit of adventure?'

I knew I was supposed to be excited. I sat back again and let my mind wander.

⁂

I jumped out of the car as soon as we stopped. Mr Pugh got out slowly and walked around to Mum's side, nodding a little as he gave her his hand to climb out. He winked at me and touched his hat. 'Ey up, little master!' he said. The wind whipped around us, and for a moment we all just stood and stared up at the house. It was *huge*. Three floors of wood and stone, black sets of windows covering the front, small, smoking chimneys jutting out of the top. I raised my eyebrows as I craned my neck right back.

Mum laughed, then shivered. 'Just as I remember. The same

door – my word, the same paint! Nothing changes.' The front door was red, a fantastic, mad red, with a faded silver knocker shaped like a cat in the centre. She looked down at me with a smile.

'Well, come on then, inside with us! Mr Pugh, could you get the first bags?' She pulled her shawl over her shoulders as we walked up the front steps. Mum tapped the door with the back of her hand three times. She stamped her feet on the mat. 'Can't make his own family wait too long, can he?'

There was a sound from inside, a rush of paws and a small, excited bark, then a thump on the inside of the door. Mum sighed. 'He's still got that thing, then.'

'I like dogs,' I said. The dog barked and scratched at the other side of the door.

'Jasper!' came a deep, sudden shout. 'Jasper, down, boy! No clawing!' More noise, of tapping feet and a small scuffle nearby, and then with a tiny creak the door opened wide. The man standing in the hallway was holding the door with one hand, and gripping the dog with the other.

'Judy!' he beamed, smiling at Mum as he pulled Jasper back.

'Robert, it's been so long,' she said, kissing him on the cheek and bending forward to look at the dog. 'Still keeping bad company, I see.'

The man grinned and rubbed his head with his free hand. He was taller than Mum, but with the same dark hair, the same brown eyes. 'You know how it is, I get attached. And this . . . !' he said, turning his eyes to me, 'this is my nephew! It must be. He looks just like me, but much more handsome. Oli, right?'

'Nice to meet you, Uncle Robert,' I said. He shook my hand and laughed loudly as Jasper pulled against his collar, trying to lick us. Mum rolled her eyes and stepped into the house.

'Don't make us wait out here in the cold, Rob.'

'I've done enough waiting of my own, you know,' he said. 'But you're both welcome here for as long as—'

'As long as we can,' said Mum. 'Busy days, you know how it is . . .'

'Well,' said Rob. 'All back together again, now.'

'Together. Yes . . .' said Mum. She snapped her head up. 'Mr Pugh's getting the bags. Help him, would you, Rob?'

'Certainly, ma'am!' said Uncle Robert, clicking his heels together and saluting at a funny angle.

As soon as he was free Jasper jumped up at Mum, crouched down, sniffed her skirt. 'Come on, Oli,' she said, calling me in. She laid her hand on my shoulder and led me down the corridor. 'Let me show you your bedroom.'

⁂

That first night was hard. The dreams were rough. I faded in and out of sleep, running from shadows and noise. I heard Mum's voice drifting through the house, and a telephone ring, and a sob, and raised voices. It was later that Uncle Rob looked round the door, and stood for a moment when he thought I was asleep. 'Poor lad,' he said, 'and bad times.'

I frowned and ignored him and fell back asleep. I dreamed, and something shifted, maybe, somewhere in the dark.

TWO

He laughed the first time I told him that nobody believes in fairy tales.

'You think stories are lies?' he asked.

'They're not, then?'

'Ha! Spittle-mouse. Shows what you know.'

We looked at each other, me and Eren. He grinned and rustled his wings. 'I'm hungry,' he said. 'I need a story.'

'Tell me one then.'

He cocked his head to one side and chuckled. 'That's not how I work. I'm hungry. Behave!'

I shivered in the wind. The open window showed the town below, and the forest that stretched over the hills. The moon was the yellow of butter. 'I don't know any good stories, still,' I said.

He smiled, let his eyebrows jump up and down on his forehead, clicked his teeth. 'I can wait.'

'How long?'

'Till the end,' he said. 'What did you think? Till the end, of course.'

8

A KNOCK ON the door woke me up the next day. I groaned, annoyed at being disturbed. I rubbed my eyes and peered out from under the duvet. Aunt Bekah came in, carrying a mug of tea. 'Morning, slugger,' she whispered, moving over to the bed and putting the tea down on the side table. 'Thought you'd need this. How're you doing? Good sleep?'

We'd met briefly the evening before. She was pretty, I guess, for an aunt. She had black hair pulled back in a ponytail and she smiled even when she wasn't talking. I liked her. Rob had introduced us with a big grin on his face. 'My pride and joy, my angel!' he'd said. 'The only sane one here!'

I sat up in bed and stretched my legs out. 'Morning.'

'Best not sleep in too long. Your mum needs you around right now.'

'Why, what's up?' I said. 'She sick?' Mum really hated travelling. It always did this to her.

'Sick? No, no – I just meant, 'cause your dad isn't here.'

We stared at each other for just a second.

I bent my wrist back and forth and sat up more. The leaves outside rustled and hissed in the breeze. 'He had to stay in London. He had something to sort out at work. He's coming soon, though,' I said.

She tilted her head to one side. She was playing with her hair, twisting it round her fingers. I could smell her shampoo. It smelled good.

'Yes, your mum said as much. So, he's staying. Right.'

'For a bit,' I said.

'Yeah.'

9

She smiled again, showing more teeth, and walked out. I fell back into the pillows.

Uncle Rob was waiting at breakfast. Bowls of steaming porridge were already on the table. 'Oli!' he said, clearing his throat with a fist to his mouth.

I wasn't in a talking mood. I sat down.

'I know everything is new, right now,' said Rob. 'You'll be back in London before you know it. Just think of this as a holiday.'

I stopped staring at my bowl and looked at him. *A treat*, Mum had called it. She said it would be fun. We just took off. I never even told my mates.

'We had to leave pretty quickly,' I said. 'I didn't bring much stuff.' I stirred the porridge with my spoon.

'Whatever clothes or books you need, we can buy them here. It's not *such* a dead place, Oli!'

Neither of us spoke for a bit. Uncle Robert drank coffee. It smelled bitter and strong. I ate some porridge, and nibbled at a sausage. At home Mum normally gave me cereal.

'Do *you* know when Dad's coming?' I asked.

Rob frowned. 'No,' he said. 'But you mustn't upset your mother by being sad that he's not here. Right?'

I looked at him. 'Sure,' I said.

'Hey, you're going to be fine,' he said. 'Lots of things to do. Explore the town, if you want. You saw the forest on the drive up here? There's a good place for a lad to roam around. The house is in pretty good order. Not like in your gran's day, but . . . yes, it's going well. It's good to have a youngster around again.'

He pushed his chair out and picked up the papers. 'And I'm

here if . . . well. Yes. I'm just here.'

That was how it was done. I was part of the house now, with Mum, and Bekah, and Jasper the badly trained dog. We unpacked our cases, fitting clothes into the wardrobes Rob could spare. Our toothbrushes went in a cup in the bathroom. Mum's books lay on the tables, spilling down the stairs and into the hall. Our stuff reached out and filled the house.

Mum was with Bekah in the garden, sipping tea, feeding breadcrumbs to birds, chatting about Bekah's paintings. After a while she sat back, humming in the sunlight, resting like some giant cat.

'So how long we here for?' I asked.

'Not now, Oli, love. Not now.'

Back inside, Uncle Rob was playing the piano. The misty notes rose up, gliding through the air, dissolving away. I found a pack of cards and built a flimsy house on the rough carpet. The jacks were all missing, and the queen of hearts.

Mum came in. She watched me.

'It's a beautiful day!' she said. 'The air's so fresh compared to London. Want to head to the park?'

'Who with? I don't *know* anyone here.'

'Oh, Oli . . .' A clock rang out for eleven o'clock. From a window by the piano I could see the garden and the wind chimes that rustled and shone.

'You mustn't mope,' said Mum. 'It's not all about just you.'

'How come we never came here before?'

'Oh, *Oli*, for goodness' sake. You know how busy your father and I are. We haven't had time. Now we do. You should be glad to get to know Rob. It took guts to move back here. Lots of memories. By the end, your gran was . . . she was weak. Rob did lots of caring for her. You give him time, OK?'

'It's not him,' I said. 'He's cool. But I'm bored. This—'

'No,' she said, cutting me off. 'No complaining. Grow up a bit, Oli, and just . . . just *cope*, for now, OK? Just . . . for me,' she added softly. I opened my mouth, stopped, and nodded.

'We're here for a holiday in the countryside,' she said. 'A nice, relaxing break.'

───

I explored. Downstairs the rooms were busy and small, filled with books and photos and tables and junk, bits and pieces from other people's lives; old, dull plates and mad, colourful paintings. Uncle Rob had given them names: the music room, the drawing room, the library, mostly as jokes to amuse himself. He kept one room without a name. The nothing room. It was dusty and empty and unheated, left without any stuff in. 'I never draw in my drawing room,' he said, 'but sometimes I *do* do nothing in my nothing room. It's really quite relaxing.'

Upstairs only had four rooms: Robert and Bekah's, Mum's, mine and a spare. Mine was the smallest, but it still beat what I was used to in London. That was good at least. Out of the window, which was tall and thin, like a glass pillar set into the wall, I could see the forest. The hills went up, away from the town, so the pine trees came to a peak far up in the sky and looked like a wave ready to break and crush the house. On that first night I'd kept the curtains pulled open wide and sat with my head on the glass, just staring up at the stars. In London you can't really see stars any more – all the city lights wash them away like paint being dipped in water – but the stars in that window were huge and clear, crowded together above me, flickering like candles, on and off, on and off, all night. I felt almost impossibly small.

The house had a third floor as well.

That was where I found him.

Uncle Robert showed me how to get up to the attic. You had to open a hatch cut out in the ceiling of my bedroom with a special hooked stick, then draw down a ladder. 'Good for catching beasties!' he laughed, pulling a face like a gargoyle.

Mum was standing in the doorway, watching and resting her hand on Jasper. 'I still don't see why you're going up,' she said, scratching at Jasper's forehead. He looked happy with that.

'Come on, Judy, the boy wants to explore! It's a good house for that. You must remember when we were littler.'

'Younger, perhaps,' said Mum. 'There's nothing up there, though. Nothing but dust and cobwebs, I'll bet. Seems like a lot of hassle. *Messy* hassle.'

'A lot of hassle? Heavens above, Judy. How old're you, Oli?'

'Twelve,' I said. I watched him hook the ladder.

Uncle Robert nodded triumphantly and patted my shoulder. 'Exactly. Twelve-year-old boys must explore the attic of any house they're in. It's a rule. Like, trousers should have their knees worn out within a single year. Or . . . brushing your teeth is important, but only when other people tell you to.'

'Rob,' sighed Mum, and she scratched Jasper harder. He looked like he liked that, too.

'It's fine, Mum,' I said. 'I promise to brush my teeth. Uncle Robert said that from up here you can look out and see the road stretching down to London. Said you used to do it all the time when—'

Uncle Robert coughed nervously, the stick in his hands hanging in the air. His back went tense, and he turned to Mum. She looked at him coldly. 'It's just a saying, eh, Oli,' said Rob. 'You'd not really be able to *see* London.'

'I know,' I said, 'I'm not stupid. I just—'

'No one needs anything from London, for now,' said Mum, patting Jasper away with the back of her hand. 'The road doesn't need *watching*.'

'I *know*,' I said again. 'I just want to see what's there.'

'Hmm,' she said, but her eyes didn't leave Uncle Robert. Then, with a flick of her skirt, she walked away. The thud, thud, thud of her shoes on the stairs echoed in the cold. Uncle Robert looked at me and gave an empty smile. 'I . . . I'd better go and talk to your mother. Here,' he said, yanking the cord that had dropped down, and pulling the ladder down on sliders that squeaked badly. 'Here, you can climb up. Be careful of the dust, and if you come back down before I'm here, remember, climb backwards, yeah?'

'Sure.'

'Good lad!' He ruffled my hair, and went off after Mum.

I watched him go and looked at Jasper, who was turning his head to the side and panting. 'Pretty much how I feel,' I said, and turned back to the loft. The black square in the ceiling had a shaft of light coming down from some window higher up in the house, and bits of dust were circling round and round. I started climbing the ladder. The cold metal felt like bites on my palms.

THREE

'Is that how you remember it?' he asks me. 'The ladder was cold? The dog was panting?'

'Sure,' I say with a shrug.

'Hmm. How about your feelings?'

'What kind of feelings?'

'Were you happy? Sad? Hungry? Weren't you curious about your mama, why the road to London made her suddenly . . . change?'

'I'm not stupid. I knew why. I just . . . I didn't want to think about it.'

Eren wags a finger and tuts. 'No, good stories need lots of thinking. About things you don't want to think about. Grief. Anger. Love! Hate, of course, is best, but you're a bit young.'

'I just wanted to go into the attic.'

'To see what you could see.'

'Yeah.'

'You found me, of course.'

I pause, suddenly worried. Is this a trap? I never know. 'I found you . . .' I repeat. It's like a dream. Did this happen?

'Well, actually, I found you,' he says, smiling. I shake

16

my head to dislodge a thought, but he just stares at me with amber eyes. 'That's how it should work,' he says.

'You found me . . .' I say, confused. I feel like I've forgotten something.

He found me. That's right. Yes . . .

'You opened the loft, see,' says Eren. 'Pandora's box. You broke the seal! The cat's out of the bag now, boy. We were destined, you and I, after that.'

I'D ONLY taken a step when someone downstairs screamed. The sudden noise shot through the house like a crack through glass.

'Bekah?' shouted Uncle Rob. His feet were pounding on the stairs.

'What's wrong?' called Mum. I jumped off the ladder and ran through the corridor, listening out for the others.

'Sweetie?' said Uncle Rob. His voice was worried. I took the stairs two at a time and found where they were standing. Bekah looked embarrassed, one hand resting on her chest, breathing deeply and leaning against the wall. Uncle Rob had his hand on her shoulder. Mum stood nearby looking nervous.

'Sorry, guys!' said Bekah with a tiny laugh. 'Don't know what happened. Didn't mean to scare you all!'

'What's wrong?' asked Mum.

Bekah shook her head. 'Oh, nothing, nothing. Just startled myself in the mirror.'

An old, bronze mirror hung on the wall next to them. Bekah

gave it a flick with a fingernail.

'I was just walking past and I guess the light was wrong. I was sure I saw something behind me . . .'

'Ghosts in the mirrors, eh?' said Uncle Rob. Mum frowned.

'No,' said Bekah, standing straight again and rubbing the glass pane gently. 'No – it wasn't a trick. It was something, I don't know . . .'

Her voice was quiet and strange. She was peering into the frame, searching behind her own reflection, like someone searching for a long-lost memory. Uncle Rob gave her shoulder a squeeze. She leaned forward and looked deeper.

'Just a shadow,' said Mum. 'Come on, no need to worry.'

'No. I mean, I *saw* something behind me, flying,' she said.

'What *was* it?' I asked. 'What did you see?'

Maybe this house wasn't so boring, I thought. Maybe there was a ghost.

Mum opened her mouth to say something, but she stopped herself and waited. We all watched Bekah, watching the mirror.

'A *bat*,' she said in a whisper. She turned to look at the wall behind us. In the mirror it reflected back, empty and dull.

'There's a bat in the house? Cool!' I said. My friends'd go mental if they heard I'd captured a real live bat.

'Well,' said Rob, 'that's it. I'm married to a madwoman. There's no bats in the house, and there's no magic mirror, either,' he added, tapping Bekah on the head.

She shook her head and looked away from the walls. 'No, you're right. Silly thing. Maybe I should drink less coffee.

I swear, I saw it, but . . . Less coffee it is.'

'Or more?' said Mum with a smile.

'You should lock me up in the attic, Rob,' said Bekah.

'Best place for madwomen. And bats. Did you get your head up there, Oli?'

I looked up the stairs as I answered. 'I was just going up when I heard Bekah shout.'

'Ruining the boy's adventures, wife!' said Rob. She stuck her tongue out and punched him lightly on the chest.

There was a dull thud and a crash in the kitchen. Mum jumped and turned around.

'What the—?'

'What was *that*?' said Bekah.

'Sounded like a window,' I said. 'Like when a football hits one. I did that in school . . .'

'Oh, yes,' said Mum slowly. 'Several times, I remember.'

We rushed to the kitchen, looking around, but everything was quiet and still. A clock on the table ticked softly. Everything looked normal – the window, the plants outside, the sink underneath – but Bekah nodded her head towards the glass.

'Look at that,' she said. 'See those marks? Like oil stains on the window?'

I moved next to her and squinted in the light.

'Feathers on the glass,' I said.

'A bird must've whacked into the window. I bet it's still alive,' said Rob. 'I'll go check outside and see.'

'Flew into the window?' asked Mum, resting her hands on my shoulders. 'How'd it do that? It's a very weird angle.

I wonder what it saw?'

'What kind of bird? It looks *massive*,' I said. I wasn't joking, either – the marks on the window were huge, the wings spread open like the flag of an old Roman soldier, stamped across the glass. Rob came back in from the garden.

'No sign of a body,' he said. 'Looks like it got away. I'm sure we'll get the bugger next time!'

'Poor guy,' said Bekah.

'You mean Rob or the bird?' asked Mum.

'Very funny, sister,' said Rob. 'But I'm not the one seeing bats in the mirrors.'

Mum looked between them and laughed. 'I see we've got an interesting summer coming.'

'The very best kind!'

'Oh, good.'

We all fell silent. Somewhere a clock was chiming. Bekah checked her watch and leaned on the table. 'Maybe . . . maybe some fresh air'd be nice. Think I'd like to get shot of this place just for a bit.'

'Could be good,' said Mum.

'Want to give us a hand with the shopping? I can show you around, if you like. You can check out where things are.'

'The menfolk will stay here and guard!' said Rob.

'Hush, dear heart. We know.'

Rob slapped my shoulder. 'We'll make fire!' he said. 'We'll kill mammoth.'

'I think maybe Oli should come,' said Mum. She knelt down and touched my face, looked into my eyes. 'It'd be good for both of us to know our way around.'

'Mum,' I said.

'Please, Oli.'

'Boy's got to explore,' said Rob, but Mum hushed him with a look. *I want to be left alone*, I thought.

I thought about the loft and the dark and the cold.

'Well, why don't we all go then?' said Bekah. 'It'd be good to be out of the house, don't you think? You two apes can carry the bags.'

'Heavy things!' shouted Uncle Rob, throwing his arms up high. 'Heavy goods!'

'I think getting out'd be best,' said Mum.

I looked across at Bekah. She was staring at the window, lost for a moment in the echoes of the feathers. She shook her head and rubbed her eyes.

'Not really spooked, are you, pet?' asked Rob. He rubbed her shoulders with a frown.

'Hmm? Oh, I'm fine. It's just . . . that bat in the glass. Gave me a fright. Nothing, really. We all off, then?'

'Looks like,' said Rob.

I tried to smile at Mum.

A treat of a visit, she'd said.

You liar, I thought.

⁂

What did I care about shopping? We moved through the aisles, choosing fruit, squeezing bread. I stole a grape and chewed it slowly, picking seeds out of my teeth. Bekah showed Mum where

21

things were. I kept quiet, hands in my pockets. It was all wrong, all strange. I hated the grubby floor, the food I didn't recognise. Cans stood in columns on the shelf. I thought about knocking them over, bowling them down with a big, sticky melon. Mum chatted and laughed and moved through the store.

We got all the bags back to the car. 'Enough to feed an army,' said Uncle Rob. 'Enough to feed one boy for one day!'

He turned the key and the engine roared. 'Off we go!' he called out.

'Wow, wait!' said Bekah with a gasp. A cat, black and shining, had jumped from nowhere onto the bonnet of the car, its tail held high and its shoulders hunched and quivering as it glared at us through the windscreen.

'Ha!' I said, leaning forward and clicking my fingers. 'Here, cat. Come on!'

'Oh, Oli, don't,' said Mum. I ignored her.

'What *is* going on today?' said Rob with a quick laugh. He tapped his knuckle against the glass. The cat hunched forward and opened its mouth in a lazy yawn.

'Beep the horn,' said Bekah.

'Here, cat, c'mon!' I whispered, sucking in my breath against my teeth, trying to make it stay. The cat pounced forwards, up over the window, landing with a tiny click on the roof.

'Flipping thing!' said Rob, sounding the horn and revving. 'It can jump off on its own, don't worry.'

'Aw, you'll give it a fright!' said Bekah. Above us the cat's claws clicked as it shifted its weight.

'Oh, I'll give *it* a fright, eh?' said Rob. He moved forward slowly and I turned in my seat to watch for the jumping cat. We were getting faster. Uncle Rob kept checking his mirrors. We all kept listening for meows. Sharp claws clicked on the roof.

'It's not off yet,' I said. 'Can't we stop and see?'

'Might be best,' said Mum.

Rob frowned. 'Fine, fine,' he said. 'Hop out, dear nephew. Give the beast a poke.'

We stopped again. I clambered out, looking around. The roads were empty, the gardens bare.

'Don't let it scratch!' called Mum from inside.

'He's gone,' I said, looking around. I *swear* I'd heard him right there, right in front of me.

I walked backwards, making sure I could see. Up and down the street, nothing moved.

'Hop back in, Oli,' said Rob. 'Let's get off.'

A gust of wind had started to blow, stirring up bits of leaves and dust from the ground. I raised my hand to my eyes, shielding them from the churning dirt. I could see something moving up ahead.

'What's that?' I said, pointing. The others followed my hand, peering ahead to see. Uncle Rob leaned against the steering wheel and stared.

Pages and pages of books were blowing down the street towards us, all torn and broken, fluttering and rustling along. Ten, twenty, soon too many to count, they tumbled and blew, catching on trees, sticking to the road and then getting swept up again in tiny, dying twisters. I stepped forwards. The paper

danced around my feet, wrinkled against the windscreen of the car, caught on my chest. They were old, dirty, stained pages, printed and written, readable and not. I spread my arms out and laughed.

'Oli, you nut, get in and shut the door!' called Mum. The paper was flapping and falling in the wind, moving on, pushed forward by the storm. I grabbed at a page stuck to my leg and pulled it tight, smoothing it out to read.

'Oliver, get in, now!' said Mum. I looked at her, crumpled the paper, stuffed it in my pocket and jumped back into the car. She frowned at me and muttered under her breath.

'A paper storm!' said Bekah. 'What d'you think of that?'

'A recycling bin pushed over by the wind?' asked Rob.

'Maybe a library exploded!' I said. The pages spluttered past as we started off again.

'Binmen not doing their job, I'd say,' said Mum.

Uncle Rob nodded as Bekah twisted in her seat. 'What'd you get, Oli?' she asked. I smiled, pulled the page from my pocket and read from the faded yellow sheet:

> . . . not long now. Too much sleep, that's the thing. And wasting my energy writing and blowing. Has to be more, going in and not out. In and not out – up and not down! Up, up, up, like . . . like . . . who goes up? Somebody does. I know, I know! Jack, and the beanstalk. Jill, to get water! Someone up a mountain? People always do. Truth and hope and answers, all up.

Who'd go down? Under things and underworlds.
Pah! Go up. Up and away, up in a sleigh!
That'd be Santy. Father Christmas, he goes up.
All the good 'uns do . . .

I stopped reading. 'That's mental!' I said. 'What's it from?'

'Sounds like the ravings of a loony,' said Bekah.

'It's handwritten,' said Mum, leaning over. 'Probably private. A diary or something.'

'*Go up, go up!*' I said, waving my hands about.

'*All the good 'uns do!*' joined in Bekah. She pulled a face and kept laughing.

'*If* you two are quite done,' said Uncle Rob. 'Enough loons right here to keep us going. Best throw the paper away, eh, Oli?'

FOUR

'What comes first? Stuff or stories about it?'

He looks at me with blank eyes. He sniffs the air and shuffles forwards.

'Why do you ask me that, matey boy?'

'Well . . . it matters. What came first.'

'Hoo! Such a human answer. It matters. Like it matters what was here first. You rate things wrong, that's your problem.'

'Then it doesn't matter?'

He shifts again and I'm not sure where he's gone. I turn around and try to squint through the night and the dust.

'I'll tell you an answer, if it's answers you want,' he says, somewhere. 'It was the stuff. The stuff, and then the stories.'

'Stuff, like . . . Everything? Life?'

'Or . . . maybe the stories led to the stuff. You think I know? You think I care?'

'I—'

His voice erupts in anger and heat, shaking the air, knocking me down to the floor.

'It doesn't concern me what led up to the stories.

There's nothing outside of them now! Nothing! Nothing outside!'

Suddenly I'm angrier than I've ever been. I grind my teeth and lash out at the dark. I grab at the floorboards and pound them with my fists. 'No! NO!' I shout. 'We were here first! We made you! Us, people! We made you!'

And we can end you, too, I think. I want to say it, but I don't.

⌗

Mum was upstairs unpacking the last of her things. I knocked. When she saw me she smiled, bright and eager, and I realised she'd been humming under her breath. 'Oli! How's it going?'

'Oh, yeah, it's great here,' I said, rolling my eyes. I felt angry. She shouldn't be *pretending* so much.

'I know it's just your gran's old house, but what a house, eh? I was happy here, way back. It was . . . calm. Not crowded, dirty London.'

'It's the *countryside*, Mum.'

'Yes!'

She started humming again. I clenched my fists. Deep breaths. One, two.

'Mum?'

'Yes?' she said. She was folding clothes, looking around the room. She looked so much better. Her eyes were less red.

'Nothing. Don't worry. Nothing.'

'Good lad. Hey, love, close that hatch to the attic, would you?

Dratted thing gives me a chill. It's been open all day, and the dust alone is dreadful. I don't know what Rob was thinking.'

'At least it's *something* interesting,' I muttered. She was watching me suddenly, chewing on her lower lip. She always did that when she was worried. She did it when she thought I'd heard her fighting with Dad again.

'What your Uncle Rob said about seeing London . . . you know that's silly, don't you?' she said.

'What? Of course.' I couldn't believe she thought I was so dumb.

She'd moved her eyes to the floor now, suddenly looking at something else, somewhere far away.

'It's . . . Mum, this place is boring,' I said at last. 'Maybe up there there's—'

'Oh, forget the loft, Oli!' she said, shaking her head. 'Forget that. And London. London isn't *here*. You need to live *here*.'

'I *know*!'

'Don't interrupt. You don't understand. Things are—' She stopped again and looked at me, a strange half-smile frozen on her face. She touched my cheek. I glared at her. 'We live here, for now, OK?' she said. 'London's . . . far away.'

Far away? *Far away?* Only because she'd dragged me here. Only because of her. I stepped back. One, two. I looked at the floor.

'Fine,' I said. 'OK.'

⊰⊱

In my room, the ladder was still poking out of the loft, a cold

29

draught falling from the hole in the ceiling. I pushed it closed with a grunt and threw myself down on the bed. What a joke. We lived here now? *Lived* here? I threw one of my pillows across the room with another, louder grunt. This wasn't my life. It was hers. 'At least Dad would have come exploring with me,' I muttered to myself.

I threw the other pillow.

⊰⊱

That night, in my dreams, I was running through the air. I flew across the town, the moon above me, the pine trees below. Their scent rose and caught in my lungs, fresh and sweet and bitter. I saw the roofs of the houses below me and fell through dark skies with the wind screaming in my ears. I saw the red door of Uncle Rob's house and heard the wind roar as I circled lower and lower. I was moving, changing, half awake and dreaming again. Then I was in the attic. There was a huge, half-circle window, the glass turned brown with dust. I watched the pines in the hills sway and creak. The road led off to London. There were boxes in the attic too, and old, silly things. A broken wardrobe, Christmas baubles, some books.

And then there was him.

He was standing behind me as I looked out of the window, waiting for me to turn around.

And I did.

I was awake. The pillow was falling off the bed. I could hear Mum talking in a room below, saying something over and over again. Rob spoke back and glasses clinked as they drank.

Sinking deeper into the bed, I fell asleep again.

The thing – was he a bat? – was too huge to see. His wings merged into the shadows, his shape too fuzzy to make out. He grinned at me with small, sharp teeth and darkness whirled around him. He cocked his head and bowed it slightly. 'Once upon a time,' he said, 'a boy dreamed, and all his wishes came true. Once upon a time, old things woke up, and magic – *real* magic – came back into the world.'

Wind was blowing all around us now, and the walls of the attic were falling away, crumbling and flaking like old, dry leaves. The thing laughed and its eyes shone yellow. 'Worlds to make,' it said, 'and worlds to take. Fly while you can, boy. *Enjoy* the power of your dreams! But remember, yes? And come back. There's so much we can do together.'

And then it was gone, swirling away with everything else into the wind and the shadows and the roaring as the world shattered into dust and noise. I opened my mouth to call out, and then I was falling too, tumbling and turning, my breath caught in my throat.

The noise from downstairs woke me up. Mum and Rob were still awake, talking late into the night. My ears were ringing with the roar of the dream. I shook my head and turned over. I felt like I was forgetting something. I thought about Dad. I closed my eyes and wished to the night for him to come soon.

The next day I walked to the shops, and that's how I met

Em. She was sitting on a red-brick wall ahead, kicking her legs up and down, tapping a stick. I kept my head down, hands in pockets, pulled my hood up against the cold, leaned forward. I wanted to pretend I wasn't there. She watched me pass, sucking her lower lip, and I heard the stick clatter as she tossed it aside. She was wearing flip-flops that slapped on the pavement like little cracks of gunfire when she ran. 'Hey, you come from number thirteen?' she asked.

I turned, not sure who she was talking to. 'Eh?'

'Thirteen,' she said. 'You come from number thirteen?'

She was younger than me, I thought. Smaller, anyway. A silver dove brooch was pinned to her chest and a pair of mad pink glasses rested just under her chin, tucked into her top. She smiled, and her green eyes crinkled.

'What d'you mean, thirteen?'

She turned her head to one side and raised her eyebrows. 'House number. Sorry, I thought I saw you going into the Talcotts' place . . .'

'Oh, no, yeah, you did. You did. My uncle's house,' I said.

She stuck her hand out. Her purple nail varnish was chipping away. 'Pleased to meet you. I'm Em.'

'Oli.'

'You here with your parents?'

'My mum.'

She sucked in her mouth and nodded slowly. 'Newbie, huh? 'Mazing. Hey, you want to see a dead crow?'

'A . . . what?'

'A crow. *Caw, caw!*' She tucked her bent elbows into her

body and batted them up and down.

I stared at her, not sure what to do. 'Where do you live?' I asked.

'Here. There. Why not? We're neighbours. That's mine,' she said, pointing to a house further down the street. 'I know Mr Talcott. My dad was best man at his wedding to . . . is it Becky?'

'Bekah,' I said, 'my aunt. Yeah.'

I looked down. I could feel her eyes on me.

'A dead crow?'

'Yeah, come on, he's just in my garden.'

We walked back past Uncle Rob's place together. I could see Mum's shadow in the kitchen window but my eyes kept moving up, all the way, to the loft. I had the feeling that I was forgetting something.

'It's really sad,' said Em. 'Maybe a cat got it. Crows are huge! Wait till you see. I took some feathers I found on the grass.'

'Um,' I said. 'Right.' The loft window was black and empty. My stomach felt strange.

I looked back at Em, drew my mind away. 'Sorry. Feathers? Is it magpies who have the black ones that are really blue and green?'

'Sure,' said Em. 'Why not? But they're half white, too. This is a crow.'

She led me into her garden, a mess of bushes and crumbling apple trees. 'Isn't it cool?' she said. 'There was an orchard here, and when they built the houses, they all got apple trees left over. One by one the other houses all cut them down, or made *patios* or *decks* or whatever. The people in this house didn't,

33

and neither will we. These trees are so old!'

They did look old; the bark was dry and knobbly and they twisted and turned like bent old men laughing in the cold. 'Can you eat them?' I asked. I didn't know what else to say.

'Yeah, we make pies!' she beamed. She skipped along the grass and bent down near a bush. 'The crow's down here,' she said.

I walked over and looked. It was big, she was right, but it was broken and battered, lying on the soil. Its beak looked like plastic, its wings hard and brittle. Nothing soft at all. She was watching me, waiting to see what I thought.

'It's gross,' I said.

'I know, right? But it's sad.'

I looked at the crow's sharp claws. It looked like a joke, but I stared. I thought something was moving deep in the darks of its eyes. A fleck of light, or a spark. I leaned in again, kneeling on the grass this time. I could swear something was shining in the sockets. I felt hot and strange. My mouth tingled. Em's smile froze at the corners of her mouth.

'You all right?' she said. 'You look kind of pale.'

I flicked my head, trying to dislodge something, trying to remember a dream or a song from long ago. Then, like a flash it came: *Eren*.

I whispered it to myself. '*Eren* . . .'

Em looked at me. 'Huh?'

I stood up. 'Eren,' I said.

'Uh, no, *Em*,' she giggled, 'for Emma.'

'What? No . . . it's . . . Sorry.'

She looked at me oddly. 'You OK? Your eyes are kind of . . .

bright.'

'What?' I said again. I shut them tight. Two pinpricks of starlight burned in the darkness. I opened them again. 'Is there something in there?'

She laughed. 'You're kind of odd, you know.'

'Um. Look, maybe I should head off,' I said, moving back to the road. Em walked after me.

'Sorry, I didn't think . . . it is kind of sad, isn't it? That it's dead, that it's the end.'

'It's not that,' I said. Would she think I was scared of a bird? 'No, it's fine. Just some dust in my eyes. Look, I'm fine.'

She opened her mouth to say something, but another voice called from inside the house. 'Ah, my mum,' she said. 'Come and say hello.'

I hesitated. 'Maybe I should go and tell Uncle Rob where I am.'

'I said they're friends. I'll get my dad to phone him.'

She ran off into the house, leaving me with the trees and the wind and the crow.

I looked up, staring at the sky. '*Eren*,' I said through my teeth.

FIVE

'Why do we tell stories?' he asks.

It's not a test, but he wants me to give him the answer. No. He wants me to give him *his* answer. But I don't know. He shakes his head and smiles his devil smile at me.

'We tell stories,' he says, 'because we know no other ways to fly.'

I remember the grass and the smell of the trees, but it's dim, like a dream, or the echo of a song. But I remember, still, a little. I remember Em and the crow. I remember Em's mum.

HER PARENTS were sitting on the sofa when we went in and they both stood up when they saw me. 'Oli, is it?' asked Em's mum. 'I'm Lucy, and this is George. Emma told us Robert's your uncle.'

'Nice to meet you,' I said. 'Yeah, me and Mum are staying with Uncle Robert for a while.'

'Ah, yes,' said Em's mum, 'of course.'

I looked at George. He nodded and smiled briefly before

turning to Em. 'You mustn't disturb the boy too much, Emma. No doubt he's got stuff to do, people to talk to.'

'Honey . . .' said Em's mum. Em's dad grunted, nodded again and sat down to turn on the TV. 'Right, well then, why don't we get you a drink? Oli, George'll phone your uncle.'

'Thanks,' I said, looking at Em. She shrugged and mouthed to me, *Don't worry about him*. In the kitchen her mum gave us each a glass of Coke.

'Don't you think Dad was being strange?' asked Em.

Her mum looked thoughtful and spoke slowly. 'I'm sure it's nothing. You mustn't worry about it, Oli. You've got friends here. Your whole family has.'

'Do you *know* Oli?' Em looked at me suspiciously and sucked her Coke through a straw.

'Don't be silly, of course not!' said her mum.

Em turned to me. 'Who are you? What government do you work for?' she said, pointing her fingers at my head like a gun. 'Pow!' she said.

'If I told you, I'd have to kill you.'

'Hey, you've got a mysterious one here, Em,' said her mum. 'You be careful. Don't let him get hold of your fingerprints.'

'Luce!' called Em's dad from the living room. She tutted and left.

'That,' said Em, 'was kind of strange.'

'Yeah,' I said. The ice in my Coke bobbed and turned. The light made it look like two eyes.

'You should meet Takeru,' she said. She sounded very certain.

'I should meet who?'

'Takeru. He's a friend. He's Japanese but he was adopted by a married couple and now he lives here. He's great!' The Coke fizzed on my tongue and tasted sweet and cold. Takeru? Sure, why not, I thought, I don't want to go back to the house. I shrugged. Em stood up and raced off after her mum. I played with a beer mat on the table, flipping it over and over. 'OK, we're ready!' said Em as she walked back in. 'Tak only lives in the next street along, but we can push through the fence down the garden to his place. Come on!'

She was already out the door and I hurried after her, leaving my drink half finished. Back outside I felt the hairs tingle on my neck as I thought of the window looking down from Uncle Rob's.

I couldn't say how, and I couldn't say what, but I knew – *I knew* – that something was watching.

I ducked my head, not looking behind me. Em raced through the garden, past the apple trees, and came to a thick scramble of trees and bushes at the bottom. Behind it, separated by an old wooden fence, I could see the roofs of a line of houses. 'Mind the holly,' said Em, 'and watch out for spiders, they seem to like it here.'

'We're going through this?' I asked.

'Man, come on. Takeru's 'mazing, you'll see!'

She crouched down and moved slowly, pushing leaves aside, working her way between branches like a cat, never letting her knees touch the ground, snaking and winding gracefully. I stumbled after her, catching my hair in the spikes, scratching through the leaves, my fingertips soon dirty and black. The fence was spotted green and purple with lichen and age. 'Magic time,' said Em, grinning like a wolf. She pushed the fence lightly with her fingertips. A small, wonky door had been cut into the fence, a gold hinge screwed onto one side to keep it in place. It opened silently, nothing more than Em's touch pushing it out, and hung limp against the other side of the fence.

'That's . . . wow, that's pretty impressive!' I said.

Em tutted and rolled her eyes. 'Pretty impressive? It's amazing! We fixed it up so we can go from his to mine to his. Like a cat flap. But an us flap!'

'Does anyone know?'

'*Them?* No!' She fixed me with a serious stare. 'You're not going to tell anyone . . . *are* you, Oli? I only just met you. I hope I can trust you with this.'

I held up my hands and flicked a ladybird off my thumb. 'Hey, this is epic. Not a word, I promise.'

She held my gaze for a few seconds more, huddled down in the soil as the sunlight flitted across the dark. Then she whistled long and low. 'Let's go!'

She scrambled across and onto the grass, beckoning me through with a wave of her hand. Then, carefully and slowly, she pushed the secret door closed, wedging it firmly back in place. The wood was rough, all thick grain and knots, and stuck in without a lock. 'Perfect, right?' said Em, and we stood up to look around.

'Won't . . . uh . . . won't his parents notice you're here?'

'*We're* here, you mean,' she said as she started walking over the lawn. I paused and looked back. The trees were tall enough to block out Uncle Rob's house; nothing in there could see us. Why was I nervous?

I couldn't stop thinking about the window.

SIX

He's happy. I can tell. He's mental and he's happy that I'm here.

'So much to learn,' he says. 'So much to do!'

'Why do you care about me?' I ask, breathing deeply, holding his stare. He tilts his head and rustles his wings in a shrug, as if he doesn't understand.

'A better question,' he says, holding up a single finger, 'would come if we shift the focus a bit. Why, young Oli, did nobody else care? Eh? Mummy and Daddy and everyone else, running around and pretending everything was so important.'

'I—'

'No, no, don't you pretend as well. Not with me. Stories I love. Pretending I hate. Stories are truths. Pretending is nasty lies! So, no. You be honest. Why didn't all them grown-ups listen to you?

I can't answer him. My eyes are burning.

'I listen,' he says, singsong and gentle, swaying his head and hugging himself. 'I always listen to the young and the lost. La, la, laaa, but I do!'

41

B Y THE side of the house we stopped for Em to pick a pebble from the path. 'Long way up, short way down,' she said, and chucked it up at a window above our heads. There was a click, a thud, a muffled voice, and then a boy's head popped out. 'Em!' he said, and then when he saw me, 'And someone else! What's up?'

He disappeared inside again and Em pushed me further along the alley, round to the front. 'Can't keep him waiting, hurry it up!' she sang, tapping the backs of her fingers on my jacket. From inside the house we could hear the sound of feet on stairs, then the front door opened with a rattle. 'Em!' said the boy, smiling widely and pushing back hair from his eyes. He leaned against the doorframe, crossing his arms.

'Takeru, I want you to meet Oli.'

'Oli, nice to meet you.'

'Good to meet you, Ta . . . um . . .'

'Takeru, silly!' said Em, punching my arm lightly. She laughed and looked at him.

'*Takeru*,' he said again. 'Don't worry. Coming in?'

'Yeah, course!' said Em loudly, pushing past him and disappearing into one of the rooms. She must've known the house well.

'Uh, thanks,' I said, feeling awkward as the boy moved past to let me in. I slipped off my muddy trainers. 'So, you know Em well?' I asked.

'Oh, yeah,' he said. 'You new here?'

'I only met her this afternoon.'

He looked sympathetic and sucked in his breath, scratched his head. 'Yeah, you kind of have to just go with it. She'll drag you along on her mad ideas.'

42

'Come *on*,' came Em's voice from inside. Takeru shook his head and led me to the living room. Em was curled up on a giant red sofa like a cat, flicking through TV channels aimlessly, the static filling the air with scratches and hisses.

'Em, what are you looking for?' asked Takeru, moving a cushion and pointing for me to sit down. 'You want a drink?' he asked.

'No, no, I'm good.'

'*Em*, what you looking for?'

'Cartoons, cartoons, cartoons!'

'Figures. Drink?'

'Yup! Got any milk?'

He sighed, raised his eyebrows at me and shook his head. 'I'll be right back, Oli,' he said, and went out. The channels fizzed and raced as Em ran through the programmes, searching for something she knew. She muttered under her breath, 'Come on, come on . . .'

I watched her, watched the TV, heard Takeru clinking glasses somewhere else in the house, felt the unfamiliar sofa with my hands.

'Whoa, stop!' I yelled, pointing at the TV.

Em jumped in her seat like a startled rabbit. 'What, what's wrong?'

The door opened and Takeru came back in. 'What you doing, what's up?'

'The TV, what channel was that?' I asked. My voice was too loud. I could hear the blood pumping in my ears, thumping like a drum in the night.

43

'What?' asked Em again, her hand frozen on the remote.

'The TV, what channel were you—? Oh, come *on*.' I yanked the remote from her, slamming the channel button again, scrolling back, my eyes burning into the set.

'What are you looking for?' asked Takeru behind me.

There was no mistake. I'd *seen* him, right there on the TV. But all I could find now was static, with two fierce dots of light staring out at me. A soft chuckle trickled in the air.

'Don't *laugh*,' I said, angry.

'No one's laughing,' said Em in a quiet voice. The channels kept coming, but I was slowing down. Football, comedy, houses, fashion. I'd missed him.

Em was still curled up, leaning forward on the sofa, her legs hooked under her. Takeru stood between us, looking nervous.

'I thought – I thought I knew someone.'

'On the TV?'

'I—'

'It's OK,' said Em, unwrapping herself and standing up. 'Mistake, eh? Unless you know Big Bird!'

''S boring, anyway,' said Takeru, turning the TV off. 'Load of rubbish.'

'Sorry,' I said.

Cars outside sounded like laughter. The shining reflections of light in the screen still looked like eyes. But that wasn't what I'd seen. That wasn't what had made me panic.

It was Dad.

SEVEN

'Here, you see, is something I can work with,' he says. He licks his lips and then reaches over and strokes my cheek, almost kindly. I shudder. 'Shh, now, tidbit,' he says.

'Yarns and tales and the telling, they're all about unravelling the truths that life hides, you ken? It's about finding out, if a princess is locked in a tower, how would you get her down? It's about you, and the story, and where the two things meet.'

I don't know what to say. It doesn't matter. He doesn't want me to talk. Something's coming. In the space between us, motes of dust spark and the air quivers.

'Listen to my own little ditty,' says Eren. 'Let the music take away your thoughts. Once,' he says, huddling closer, 'there was a man, and he lived in a place that was dark, and cold, and fierce winters would bite at his heels. Can you feel the cold nip you? Try and close the door against it, but there's a wind that breaks through the cracks. He would build a fire to save himself every night, but it was never so strong that it could fight the dark, slow hours, and he would end up huddled near it, embers all aglow and spitting and cracking while snow drifted down the chimney. Oh, pity the man, and his burdens! The days were bright and cold, and he'd gather wood from the forests to burn that night, but never enough to see him through to the morning. The snow was soft and it crunched like a lamb's skull as he walked, and the ice was black, black and dead as the space between moon and star. Feel the darkness there, just beneath your skin, where it prickles! And so it was. Bright day always fled, tricky temptress that it is, and night howled in with wolf and frost and moon to catch you in her hands. Oh, don't trust the moon, 'cause she's a bigger tease than any, and to see her full face is to fall into the dead lake where it's reflectin'. No, don't love the moon. What was he to do, though? The embers are dying. Feel them splutter as you grasp the blanket! What was he to do? And so it was.

'The winds, you know, are brothers. The north, the south, the east, the west. All of them sons of the moon, no doubt. They never meet. Well, never, except for one time, one time every hundred years – or is it a thousand years, for this tale? – and then, beneath the heavens lit by pure starlight, they will. Starlight is so delicate, and so rare, you see. Normally the moon will not let stars be seen, properly, from down here. On this one evening, though, the moon leaves the sky, to meet the winds, and the stars sing and dance and burn. This one night, when the man would not be chased by roaming frosts, and would be free to act on his hatreds. And so it was.'

Eren is watching me as he talks, and I feel every word like a prick on my skin. I feel cold.

'The tale is over,' he says.

'What? How can it be? It can't be!'

'Ha!' he laughs, high and cackling and ancient. 'Ha, you see? You know it isn't. What story was that? You want to know more. It would drive you mad not to know. Not to know a story in this place' – he spreads one wing around me – 'would drive you mad.'

'How does this one end?' I ask. I don't have any strength to fight these games.

'I shall tell you, of course,' he says, like a kind magician finishing a trick, a king granting one last wish.

'The night came,' he says, and I feel my bones chill, hear the wind rock the forests as the moon falls from the sky, 'and the moon dropped down, buttery, milky, chalky, pasty. The winds from the four corners all came to talk, and the world, in the dark hours, was still, and cold, and silent. Can you see the stars? They dance and shine! The yellow-white moon-bulb is away, and the stars, real light, are popping and twirling and fizzing and sparkling like stars really should. Imagine the velvet sky, blue and heavy with midnight, dotted with water drops. Imagine that. Beautiful. Little did they all know, though, that man was hiding nearby.'

I see the stars. I feel the moon breathing nearby. I see the man crouched and hiding and waiting.

'What was his plan, this man, this man who was

47

hunted and haunted by those others? It was so simple. He only wanted warmth. He only wanted fire that burned into the morning. He only wanted what was right. And so it was. The moon and the winds, they were talking, and the man, he walked up to them, begging to tell them a truth! He shouted, it was urgent, they had to know what had happened. Well, you don't spend all your life looking down on everything, roaming everywhere, if you're not a curious thing. "What do you mean, what has happened?" they asked. The man bowed his head, so weak, so humble. "The South Star, I have heard, is to be made queen over the sky, and there will be no more need for a moon!"

'"What! What! Murder! Treason!" they shouted, and oh, can you see it, can you imagine the anger and horror in that white, terrible moon-face? The winds howled, roared they did, bellowed and would have torn the world apart if she hadn't spoken for quiet. The man lay down and begged his apologies. "Oh, you are a good friend, to warn us of such danger!" said them all.

'"I simply know my place," said the man, "I know my place, and I know yours as well." And so it was. The moon left early, for the first time ever from that meeting of a thousand years – or was it a hundred? – and raged to the stars, called them terrible things, and the South Star she threw to the ground, swearing the star could never return. The night air was yellow and thick with the light of a full, golden moon. The man approached the South Star as she lay, in shock, in the snow. "I have heard," he said, "what

48

has happened, and those winds had no right to do so!"

'"The winds?" asked the star. "What have the winds done? It was the moon that threw me down like a dog!"

'Do you feel her pain? She was the light of the south, a princess of the sky! Poor duckling, poor innocent, poor victim! The man spoke on. "The winds, you may know, met this very night – I heard them as I slept in my bed, frozen though I am, humble, a poor man, sleeping through this most terrible of nights . . . yet I heard them and their plotting to have you thrown down here, that they could call you their own."

'"What! What!" cried the South Star, and she burned in terrible anger. Her flames danced and licked at the ground and singed the air like lightning. "I am wronged!"

'"We both are, my lady, we both are," said the man, and he rubbed his hands in the warmth. And so it was . . .'

I can feel the warmth. Eren smiles and licks at his nose. He rocks back on his legs and wheezes and mutters. The air smells like fire and snow.

'"Come in from the cold," said the man. "Come, rest; I have no more beds, I fear, but the chimney is free, and you will be safe there from any rain."

'"Such kindness, from a stranger!" sang the star. "I am so grateful!"

'The man led the star to his house, and placed her in the fireplace, and they slept, exhausted, and dreamed. That night the wind howled strong and crept to the

49

poor man's house. It lapped at the cracks like waves of a tide, and soon the house was chilled by the gusts. The man shivered, and woke. "The wind, back to get you!" he cried to the star. The South Star rose from her bed.

Now, I take it you've never seen a star go to war? They have them, you know, wars and battles. It is a terrible sight to see, and one you would never forget. The winds are the sons of the moon, but the stars are her companions, and shine in their own right. A star may have power over a wind. The South Star burned and screamed, charged and lunged and beat the wind from the man's door, marking a line that she scratched in the earth that no wind may ever cross. The man was so pleased he wept, just a little, for joy.' He stopped again, and sighed. 'Near enough the ending for you?'

'Isn't that it? Is that it?'

'Boy, don't you learn? I will drive it into your soul. Stories don't end because they can never die. They're truer than truer than true. The South Star, what happens to her? Won't the man get found out? There's no end.'

'It never ends?'

He looks at me coldly and in his eyes something flickers, something dark and dangerous. 'Stories are different, sometimes. Do they end and die, you ask?' He pauses. 'Mine don't.'

I WALKED HOME alone, ignoring the looks I'd got from Em and Takeru, the glances that had shot between them. I knew I'd acted crazy, but I was sure. I was sure it had been my dad. The world around me was quiet, almost empty. My footsteps on the pavement clumped and died without even an echo. I thought about the loft. I thought about what I hadn't seen, and what I had. I thought about the name Eren, and mumbled it under my breath, tasting it in my mouth like a new food. My stomach rumbled even though I wasn't hungry.

The house. Herbs growing in the neat orange pots outside, honeysuckle winding its way over the walls, the tiny sound of wind chimes pricking the air. I looked up, not sure what I thought I would see, and tried to clear my head.

'Hey, Oli!' came Uncle Rob's voice from the kitchen window. 'So you found your way to old George's, huh?'

'Oh, yeah,' I said. 'Yeah, I met his daughter. She's . . . she's OK. Kind of cool. She took me to meet another friend.'

He raised his eyebrows to show he was listening and called me inside with a flick of his head. The house smelled like coffee and lemons. 'Listen,' he said as we sat at the kitchen table, 'I know you weren't sure how long you'd be here. The summer holidays are only just beginning, I know, and there're probably lots more interesting things you could be doing, but . . .'

He let the last word hang in the air. I stared and he cleared his throat nervously. 'Well, I think it's fair that you know, you'll probably stay here right up until school starts again. Your mum's not so keen to spend the summer in London, you know.'

'I saw Dad on TV,' I said, suddenly.

Uncle Rob looked at me strangely. 'Really? Are you sure? I haven't seen anything.'

He looked towards the television, then back at me, and sucked in his breath. 'I mean, why would your dad be on TV?'

'I don't know,' I said. I looked at him. He was lying. I knew they all were. I didn't know why, though. Something was wrong. 'I guess it wasn't him,' I said. 'It was, like, a millisecond anyway.'

'Oh, sure,' he said. 'Oh, I'm sure it wasn't, then. Why'd he be on there? Like you said!' He cleared his throat and put his hand on my shoulder, letting it lie there, heavy, for a moment. 'Nothing to fret about. Why don't you go and help your mum with something?'

I stayed where I was. 'How come you've never visited us in London?' I asked. 'It's huge. You could see so much more than here.'

He smiled gently, not looking at me. 'I've been to London before, Oli, don't you worry about that. I'm not some impoverished farmer who's never seen a car. I've seen London, I've travelled around. I just don't go as often as I used to.'

'Mum'd like it if you visited.'

He was watching me out of the corner of his eye, fiddling with the papers on the table. 'She . . . said that?'

I shrugged. 'You're family.'

'Maybe, then,' he said, 'I'll visit more.'

He turned away and I started to leave. 'What's *in* the loft?' I asked.

52

'Up there? Just stuff. Old boxes. Feel free to look, neph.'

I looked up, imagining myself floating through the ceiling, all the way up to the darkness.

⚒

Mum was sorting through clothes again, emptying another bag, straightening a skirt.

'I met a couple of kids who live on this street,' I said.

'Ah, good! We'll have to invite them round.'

'Nah, they know Uncle Rob already. His best man's daughter, that's who I met.'

'Oh, of course – is it Gordon?'

'George.'

'Oh, yes. I remember him. A strange man. He used to . . . cause problems, sometimes. Well, it's good you're making friends. Helps us settle in a bit.'

I sighed and knocked my shoes against the door.

'Try and keep that loft hatch closed, please, Oli,' said Mum without looking up. 'I told you the draught shoots through.'

'I closed it,' I said, shoving my hands in my pockets.

'I'll get Rob to double-check.'

'I closed it, Mum,' I said, frowning.

'Yes, love. Thanks.'

I kicked at the carpet and walked out.

⚒

I tried to sleep that night. I knew I wouldn't. The growing moon threw mountains of light up the wall, splashes of yellow that

53

melted away in the wind. I heard the door rattled by the breeze, felt the ticks of the clocks downstairs. A car alarm screamed far away. A dog barked. I looked out of the window, pulling back the curtains to watch the night. The windowpane was cold; the painted wood shone with dust. I looked at the stars, pushed higher and higher in the silence. They really did flutter, like millions of insects far away. I thought about the massiveness of space and shivered. The quiet and the stillness of the night made the trees look hard and sharp, every flick of their leaves strange, distorted, new. My breath frosting the glass, I hummed for a moment, waiting.

If I was going to go to the loft, I had to be totally silent.

I pulled down the hatch with the weird hooked pole and got the ladder down slowly, inch by inch, tiny squeak by tiny squeak. I rested its feet on the carpet and stared at the black hole in the ceiling. Dust was falling, swirling and twisting, and then nothing. I climbed. The ladder's rungs were cold through my socks. Every rung creaked. At the top I stopped again, forcing my hands up, taking a deep, empty breath before I looked in.

In front of the window, a black silhouette in the stars, something was waiting for me.

❦

EIGHT

'I'll tell you another story, for all it's worth,' he says, 'though, truth be no stranger, it's not really what I'm about. Telling them is kind of working against my nature. No matter, though. If you know how to tell 'em better after this, it's all the same to me, eh?'

He touches my chin again with a sharp claw and grins. I smile without feeling anything. No, actually, I feel tired. His voice changes and he hunches over, acting now.

'Have you heard of the selkies, boy? Bless the saints if you haven't, curse the fates if you have. I'll tell you the story of my own fall to froth, and then we shall see how you fare. My name is lost in the waves now, eroded in the sands, crushed beneath the deep places of the world, but once, so long ago, it was spoken by my people. I was a king, you know. Before the Romans tried their pomp, before the Vikings ran bloody and hungry across the fields, I was King of the North Islands and Prince of the Green Lands. I was a fool. Damn stupid. I'd heard a tale, from a traveller here or there, from the fishing tribes who lived back against the beach, of a woman, a woman so beautiful, so heavenly, that to see her was to fall in love. I was proud. I thought that I, as king, should have such a woman. Doesn't that sound right? I was king of all I could see, from the mountains that led up into the ice lands, to the flat plains that led off south, to Rome. I was right. The tales were sparse but all of them held truths, of where she had been seen, of which village, of what time. The fish-sellers in the markets were paid well for their fish and even better for their tongues if they could share with me secrets of the woman. We searched, and every day, every inn, every dirty drink I shared with murderers and traitors in dens and hives in my own lands led me closer, fed by whispers, following an ancient, lost, eternal trail. I was mad, I'm sure you'd say, and you'd laugh at my name if it wasn't lost to shells and foam, but hang your mockery now, because I found it – the town, the beach, the time, the place, the chance. Curse them all. A selkie is not a prize you win without payment. The moon rose low that night, the tide fell out, the water calm and salty, good for fish, good for catching things that slip away. I crouched, in rocks and weed, and waited for the woman, waited for the signs that I had heard, to carry out the secrets I had learned. She came, from the sea, black eyes, water hanging like diamonds on her back, smooth and calm and like a child. A selkie! A seal-wife, a seal-woman, come to land to shed her skin, and stand on two legs for just one evening. Her fur, suddenly so lifeless, was on a rock, folded away. I took it! She had no choice from then on, for I was a king, which mattered nothing to her, but I had her pelt, which was all her life. She bowed to me, and was mine. My own. My destruction, in the end. Would you tame the sea with a trick, son? Would you calm a howling, freezing wave, high as ten trees, solid as a wall, with theft? She brought with her the anger of ancient tides, the misery and loneliness of the deep. Crops failed. My people were sick. Raiders on the coast were blessed with wind and tide, while my own ships were lost in every weather. Each day she sat, my prize, beautiful, empty as a gem-studded cup, and watched my world slip under the water. I sank. I begged her, no more, said that she was to go, that I was wrong, and sorry – I threw the pelt back at her, hidden for so long where only I knew, but I threw it for her! And she took it, and slipped away, a minnow, gone through the net. A selkie. I've got no moral for you, boy. I was destroyed, and I'm long dead now. I've only got wisdom. Don't think to tame a selkie. Water is older than a man of earth could ever really know.'

I feel better, I think, after Eren's story. A selkie. The grey, rolling thunder of the waves pounds in my head, boom, boom, boom, and I stare into his eyes.

I'm in trouble.

⸙

'HELLO, BOY,' he said in a whisper. His voice was as dry as crackling flames. I climbed through and stood in the loft, staring at the monster. 'Yes, yes, come in. You've taken your time!' it said.

He was smoke, turned into a bat – or a bear, tattered and old. His face was pointed – a wolf, a rat? A vulture? – and his eyes shone, brighter than the stars far behind him. He was big, old, moving, creaking, grinning. I took one step and stopped.

'Eren,' I said.

'At your service, sir!' he said. He beamed and bowed, one wing, ending in a claw, in front of his stomach. In my mind, I saw him wearing a top hat, a fine black suit, a cane. In the attic he was dirty and pale.

'I saw you,' I said. It was all I could think of. He looked thoughtful.

He smiled, and nodded. 'Hmm. Yes. You *have* seen me, you're right.'

'You watched from here,' I said.

'In a way.'

'Who are you?'

'No,' he said, taking a step towards me. 'No, you mean *what am I*? That's what you mean, isn't it?'

My mouth was dry, my heart thumping inside my chest. He looked like a bat, except giant, huge, filling the space in front of me, grinning like a devil, wet, black nose scrunched up, brown hair dull and dusty, velvet wings and claws hooked under his arms. He was *real*. He shuffled forward, smiling. I saw his teeth again, saw them flash. 'Ah, don't worry about insulting me, boy! It's a good question, to be sure.' He turned away again, walking back to stare out into the night. 'Once there was a boy,' he said, 'who was not lonely, but did not have friends. He had friends in other places, but not in the new house, not where he was now. He was an outsider in the world, and an explorer.' His voice was deep, but not human – like an old recording of a man; metallic, somehow wrong. I stared at him. 'This boy, now, he had a purpose. He had a role. Do you know what it was?' he said.

'What are you?'

'I am such stuff as dreams are made on!'

'What?'

'I am here,' he said. He sighed, long and heavy. 'And now you are, too. How about that . . .' He sighed again. 'It's easy, to begin with. The boy had to tell stories. Good stories – enough to fire imaginations and break worlds. That is what he had to do. OK?'

I looked closer, barely breathing. And then, like a flash . . .

'My dream . . .' I whispered. His head jerked up, like he'd been shocked with electricity.

'But I'm not alone,' I said quickly. 'My family, they know, and if you—'

'I will not hurt you, boy! What is this? You came to me, remember. You climbed the ladder. I just waited. Knock knock.'

'What?'

'Jokes! Knock knock!'

Was he serious? 'Who's there?'

'Rufus,' said the monster quickly.

'Rufus who?'

'Run! Your *roof* is on *fire*! Haha!' He started laughing, clutching his stomach with his bent little hands, shrieking and gasping for breath, laughing and banging his fist on the floor.

He wiped a tear from his cheek. 'Good times,' he whispered. 'I've waited for that.'

'Eren,' I said again. He turned towards me.

'That's it, is it? My name? OK.'

'Isn't it?'

'It is indeed. You said so.'

I took another step, trying to see as much as I could of him. 'What *is* your name, then?'

He ignored me, watched the stars again, yawned. 'How are you, Oli?'

'I'm cold.'

'Yes. Yes, me too. We all have need of fire, I believe. You will be able to help me, Oli. Isn't that good?'

'Help? What help do you need?'

'I am . . . lonely. I have been here a while, with no company. We could talk . . .'

There was a small noise from downstairs, a door shutting gently in the corridor. I met Eren's beetle eyes and backed away. 'Aye me, the magic's broken, then?' he said, and slumped down against the wall. 'I won't leave the loft, so you can sleep well tonight, little friend. Dream, dream of great things. Come again!' The white dots flashed again, specks of ice in blackness, and I reached out a shaking hand to touch him. He was as cold as winter stone. With a single pull he lifted me up and guided me over to the hatch. His wing wrapped around me, smooth and dark as ink, and I shivered as it rustled. 'Once there was a boy,' he said, 'who would create worlds. Come back to me, OK? Come back some time. That's enough.'

A wisp of wind ruffled my hair, oily smoke surrounded me, and suddenly I was alone.

I could hear him even as I was climbing down the ladder.

NINE

'That's not a very flattering picture of me, is it?' says Eren. 'Oily smoke? Cold hands? A wet nose?'

I shrug. 'Does it matter now?'

'Well . . . things always matter, when they're being told. You have to describe people a certain way, or you can ruin a tale.'

'Huh.'

'You're still not sure, are you? About stories. About the telling of things.'

'What is there left for me to get?'

Eren chuckles and rolls his eyes upwards. 'You're ridiculous. Even here, you can't work things out? Keep going. Tell me again. Make me believe it.'

'I can't . . .'

'By all the clouds, boy! Keep on.'

Eren is becoming more demanding. He won't let go, any more.

⸻

I DREAMED. I walked through fields of grass on grey flint paths, watching as the sun set and purple streaks turned the sky dark. I heard the sea foaming over the hill and saw knights sleeping under the earth. I saw their swords, their treasure, their shields shining white and gold and red. I saw them waiting for a future that I'd never see. I moved on, confused and dazed, and saw a seal cross the path, as horses ran with fire under their hooves. I kept walking. I saw Mum and Bekah and Uncle Rob burying radios and burning papers, camera flashes replacing the stars. Behind me Em and Takeru watched, afraid, and called me over. I shook my head. *I had to move on*, I said. *Why would you choose to go back?*

Vines grew over libraries and turned the stone to chalky dust, and the books flew off into the night as crows. I heard a voice, far away, call my name. Dad? I ran. *Dad!* I called back. The grass was slate, crunching and loose, and I tried to scramble down without falling into the sea. *Dad!*

The slate was bats, filling the air, knocking me down and picking me up. I lost my footing, thought I would fall into the cold and the salt of the sea. I flew, carried by the bats in their thousands, over everything, into the sky, above the clouds, and suddenly it was quiet, so quiet I couldn't even imagine noise. No insects clicked, no wind puffed. The clouds were a white field under my feet, and above me, perfect night, perfect nothing. *Higher!* I said. *Higher, higher!* From far below, almost a whisper, someone was calling my name.

'Oli, wake up!'

My mum's voice from downstairs. I jerked awake, my eyes stinging in the light. It was morning already and the sunlight was pale and looked like it was floating in the air. I barely remembered getting into bed. But I knew. I *knew* now. He was

64

in the loft. He really was, the thing, that thing, whatever it was, or *he* was; was *there*. I don't know why I wasn't more scared, why I didn't tell Uncle Rob to run, to call the police, to do anything to kill it. I knew I was scared of him, knew it in the very centre of myself, but there was something more. There had to be more and I wanted to know what it was. I got up and went to find Mum. As I moved I felt tired, like I hadn't slept at all. My head hurt, and my eyes, and my legs. In the kitchen the TV was playing in the background, a bright, bubbling programme about some sort of antique hunt. Mum smiled when she saw me and handed me toast.

'Cereal's in the cupboard down here if you want it.'

'Mm. Thanks.'

'Ah, I think this is such a lovely house, y'know?' she said, resting her hands on the sink and staring out at the honeysuckle. Far off a bird sang high and clear. 'It's . . . it's old, I think that's what I like. There's real history, isn't there? And Rob's done such a good job of caring for it.'

'I like ours more, though,' I said.

'Oh, but London's so hectic and cramped compared to here.'

'It's not cramped, it's alive. We're in the countryside.'

She looked thoughtful and straightened her skirt. 'Yes. Yes, we are. But you made some friends yesterday, you said.'

'I met some kids.'

'George's girl. Yes. I'm sure she can show you the sights. The woods might be worth an explore.'

I ate the toast listening to the babble from the television.

I could ask about Dad. No, I thought, I'll wait for that. Wait until I have to. The toast tasted weird and I put it down again.

'I'm off shopping later,' said Mum. 'Anything you want? I'll get some treats. What would you like, and I'll make sure I pick it up.'

'You'll get anything?'

I made myself, *made* myself, not think about the loft.

She smiled and came over to stroke my hair. 'Oi, get off!' I flicked my head away and she ruffled the back.

'Too big for petting now?' she asked.

'Jaffa cakes,' I said.

'That's not some new cuss, is it?'

'Jaffa cakes! If you want to buy me something.'

Bekah had walked into the room, and Mum exhaled with her hands on her hips. '*If you want to buy me something* if you please! You hear that, Bekah? That's all the respect I get.'

'Have you tried ruffling his hair?' asked Bekah.

'I'm off, I'm off!' I said, cramming the last crusts of toast into my mouth and standing up. 'Jaffa cakes!' I called back into the kitchen. 'Jaffa cakes for everyone!'

The sound of laughter filled the hall.

❧

She went out with Bekah at eleven o'clock and I was left, alone, in the house. The loft was filled with light when I went up.

'It makes my old heart burst with pride,' he said, 'that you have come again.'

His brown hair was turning grey with dust. It looked faded

in the light. His eyes shone with life.

'You need to tell me more,' I said, and I heard my voice quiver. I made myself step forwards, towards him.

'Do I?'

'What are you?'

'Oh, that old chestnut. You can't understand just yet, my pet. You will get to know my ways, if you take time. For now, let me get rid of those nasty fears of yours. No, I'm not human, and no, I'm not a monster. No, I don't eat children or suck on their juicy bones, and no, I don't really want to hurt you.'

'I don't know if I can trust you.'

'My name is Eren,' he said, 'and you do trust me, if you think about it.'

His teeth flashed as he smiled and turned his head through the light. He looked around the attic. 'Aye me. This place isn't much, is it?'

'Why are you here?' I said, louder. I wanted him to go, to leave, to not exist.

He didn't move. 'Why not? Here is good. Here is good, for me.' He lowered his eyes, staring into the floor. 'Here is good,' he said again, and looked almost confused, almost uncertain. I thought of old men who had lost their memories, and for a tiny moment, felt sorry for this thing.

'What do you mean, I trust you? I don't—'

'Do you know any stories?' he said. He spoke quickly, almost as though he were ashamed, like some terrible secret, some nasty habit was being let out. He spat out the words like a cough.

'I . . . *what*?'

'Stories. Old ones. New ones. Happy ones. Terrible ones. Once upon a time, three blind mice, oh my, see how they run, and they all lived, except for one, who must avenge his father, no, I *am* your father, and I must take the sword that was broken, hickory dickory dock—'

'You're mad,' I said.

Eren stopped chattering and looked straight at me. I stepped back and gasped. His head twitched to the side, like an owl's. 'I am not mad, son,' he said. 'I am Eren. And that is what I need – stories. That is what I live on. Your blood and bones and bread and tea are all safe from me, fear not. I live on *tales*.' His eyes were wide, the corners of his face stretching as he stared at me desperately. I realised he was on his knees. He was *begging*.

'Stories are more than you people think,' he said. 'They are as brilliant as a sun. They're everything. I must have them like you need water, like birds need air, like love needs more life, like darkness needs hate, like . . . like . . .'

'Stop talking,' I said. I moved away again, but he went quiet, shuffling back to the window to stare at the world. His wings trembled. In my mind I heard his name tumbling through the silence. Eren, Eren, Eren, Eren . . .

Stories? Did I know any stories?

'Once upon a time there were three pigs,' I said. His ears pricked up and I saw his shoulders tense. My heart was like a cannon in my ears, booming and booming. 'There were three pigs, and they all . . . they all lived in a field. But a wolf, there was a wolf, and he came, wanting to eat the pigs, see? So they knew they had to build houses. One house for each of them –

they didn't like each other, I think, so one house each. Oh, they were, like, brother pigs. The first one, he says . . . uh . . . he says he'll build using straw. It's cheap, and easy to do, and I think maybe he was a farmer? A pig who was a farmer. Or he bought it cheap from a farmer. He built a house from straw.'

Eren turned to me, full on, and nodded, once. I tried to wet my lips with my tongue. My throat felt dry. 'There was a second pig, and he thought, uh, straw isn't enough. I mean, a wolf, right? He used wood. He got a bunch of wood, and he built his house, quite near to his brother's, but not, like, in the exact same place. Nice and strong, he thought – wood everything, wood doors, wood walls. All wood.'

Eren twitched his head from left to right like a curious bird watching a worm, and I felt nervous. How did the next part go? 'The third pig, he's the smart one. He knows the full strength of the wolf. "I'm not dumb," he says. "I know that it takes more than that to keep them out." He uses money, and he buys bricks, and cement, and he builds a house from those. It takes effort, and his brothers laugh at him, but he knows what he's doing, cause he's a . . . he's a smart pig.'

Eren nodded like a wise old priest and held his hands together in front of him. 'A classic flaw to be unveiled and a moral to be taught,' he said under his breath. I heard the words so clearly I shivered. 'Keep on, you are not finished!' he said.

'The wolf came,' I said, my eyes never leaving his. 'He went to the first house, and asked to come in, but the pig wouldn't let him. He knew what was coming.'

'I don't think he did,' said Eren. He was grinning. I thought he

69

looked like a toddler playing with insects, powerful and clueless.

'The wolf huffed, and puffed, and blew the house down.'

'Ha, yes, he did, that's how it happened!' said Eren in a hoarse shout, and clicked his claws.

I shuddered and tried to keep talking. 'The pig ran to his brother. They both hid in the wooden house. The wolf came again, and again, they wouldn't let him in . . .'

'Repeating the mistakes. Shows the fool,' said Eren.

'The wolf huffed . . .'

'. . . and puffed!'

'. . . and he blew the house down.'

'I'm sure they looked delicious, all pink and scared and running away.'

'They ran to the last pig,' I said. I was shivering with cold, with effort. I couldn't stop staring at his eyes. He lowered his face and waited for me to speak. 'The last house was made of bricks,' I said.

'Like this one.'

'Y-yeah. The wolf came to them.'

'Asked to be let in.'

'They said no.'

'Anyone would. And then . . . ?'

'He huffed, and puffed, but the house was strong, and they were safe inside.'

Eren sighed, deeply, and patted the side of his head. 'Brains, that last pig. Brains.'

'There's more,' I said. 'That isn't the end of the story.'

'Then, Oli, I would like to hear it later. Later, but not now.

I am too tired. You have done me such a service, such a favour. I bless you, with every wish and dream I have. Go on now. Your friend is at the door.'

I felt the air clear, as if I were falling asleep. I felt cold on my cheeks, the wood of the floor beneath me, heard the creak of the beams, the sound of birds and cars outside. I felt like I could sleep. I felt empty, suddenly; impossibly tired. Eren chuckled and moved to the shadows in the corner. 'Knock knock,' he said. The doorbell rang downstairs.

TEN

'Stories are the truth beyond the flat, stone world,'
he says. 'There's more fire inside the engine than the
wheels. That's what it is.'

'I'm cold,' I say.

'The world turns on its axis, but people turn on their
souls. Things you can't see, boy, support what you can.'

'We tell stories to fly, you said.'

'I did.'

Is he proud of me? I hope so. I want him to be.

'But you're not the same.'

He moves like a mist to be nearer to me. 'I'm not.'

'What do you need stories for? To live?'

'To live,' says Eren, and he sounds sad, infinitely sad,
a small voice lost in the night. 'Living is the strangest
story there is, boy. Try not to forget that. It's swings and
roundabouts in the end. Stories define you, but you are
the stories that matter. I'm just an outsider, in the end.'

Stories feed him. We are stories. He moves like a mist
towards me.

'Wow, you look awful!' said Em when she saw me. She was wearing a giant pink sunhat. I stared.

'I . . . I was sleeping,' I said.

'Now? Wow, you're mental. It's a great day. Come on, come and meet my friend the sun. Looks like you could do with it, you sleepy bum.'

'Yeah,' I said, dazed. The sun shone down and I almost winced. 'Yeah, let's go. Go where?'

'World's our oyster,' she said.

'The forest, then,' I said. 'Let's go there.'

We called for Takeru and all walked together to the hills. The path was old and yellow, caked mud and dust all worn flat and hard. Takeru and Em chatted and joked and I dragged along behind, hands in my pockets. The distant trees grew closer and taller, until the sky was being held up on their spiky crowns and we could see them spreading out down the hill and up again, like soldiers lined up to attack. The forest felt thick and dark. 'Wow,' I said. 'It's pretty big.'

'This is where you get Robin Hood and goblins and poor Hansel and Gretel walking around all lost,' said Em.

'All in one place, huh?' asked Takeru, smiling at me. The path turned into dry grass and rough weeds, swaying and rustling as we stamped through. Insects buzzed and seeds sprayed out in front of us. 'They've got to be old, some of these guys,' said Em, looking up at the pines. 'I mean, there's real history here – myths and all sorts.'

'Actual myths about these trees?' asked Takeru.

'Sure.'

'Why haven't I heard? You're full of it.'

'Am not. And you never asked. OK, so these aren't *famous* stories, but they're real – ancient myths, ones not meant for children and babies, Tak.'

'And you know them, eh?' said Takeru. He was walking beside me, with Em leading the way. 'She doesn't know anything,' he said in a hushed voice. I smiled. This open space was good. I felt freer.

'I *do* know them, because I bothered looking, I bothered finding them,' said Em, coming to a stop and waiting for us. Our jeans were spotted with grass and dew. The forest was black beyond the first few trees.

'Where'd you find them?' I asked. Takeru rolled his eyes and muttered something, but Em shushed him and continued.

'There's a library, and there's a society for local history – old stuff about the town. I think it's brilliant.'

'Cool,' I said. I started walking again. 'How far in can we go?' I asked. 'I mean, how far are there paths?' I imagined a wolf on our trail. Did wolves even live in England? I didn't know.

'No paths,' said Takeru, 'but it's pretty easy to walk through most of it. Gets a bit steep on the hills, though, and all the roots make it pretty tough going.'

'Come on, then,' said Em. 'In we go. Charge!' She ran, letting her battle cry echo through the air as she slipped into the shade. I followed with Takeru, running suddenly as fast as we could, clouds of grass seeds swirling in the wind. The shadow of the trees was cool and felt damp on my face.

'So go on, then,' shouted Takeru as we ran, all three of us, through the forest. 'Tell us the myths!'

We stopped, panting, each leaning against a trunk to catch our breath. The whole place smelled of earth and water and wood. It smelled real. 'How about the story of Full Lot Jack?' said Em in a dark, hushed voice, and she crept behind the tree and whispered into the knots, 'Come out, come out, Full Lot.'

'What kind of name is that?' asked Takeru.

'Come out, Full Lot, come out,' she whispered to the leaves. They sighed and danced in the low light. She smiled at Takeru and stuck her tongue out. 'It's a name you should be careful of, in these places,' she said.

'Oh, yeah?'

'It was a long time ago, I think; though maybe it wasn't, maybe it wasn't that long ago at all. There was a girl—'

'I'm sure there was,' said Takeru, looking at me.

'There was a girl and she was walking in the forest. Not at night, not being stupid, just walking, like we are, and she saw something in the trees. It was silver, and even though it was a sunny day, it was shining brighter than anything else. She went towards it. A pool! A puddle, really, not deep – but the water was so flat, so smooth, it was like a spilled mirror, like diamonds you could drink. She stared. "What makes you stare at the puddle?" says a voice behind her. Whoa! She turns around. There's a man there, dressed strangely. A foreigner, she thinks, 'cause his clothes look good, and well made, but they're still weird. "Oh, excuse me," she says, "I was just amazed by the light." He smiles. "Aye, that'd be a miracle, that. It's taken me many a moon to collect so much." "This is yours?" she asks, all impressed and astounded. "What is it?" The man looks at her, weighs her up and down in his mind, and speaks in a strange voice. The girl thinks she shouldn't be talking to such a strange man, alone in a wood, but she doesn't want to leave. It all looks so magical. "You want to know?" he asks. "It really is pretty," she says. She would like to know. So he tells her. "It's *dreams*," is what he says.'

Em paused to knock on the pine trunk and call into the hollows. Takeru snorted and clicked his tongue, but I was listening.

'"Dreams? How does someone take dreams?" asks the girl. "Oh, you don't take them. You are given them, by those who are good and honest enough."' When Em spoke as the man her voice was low, like the growl of a dog. It made me shudder.

'"Why would a person give up a dream?" "Oh, for a greater prize," he says. The girl can't stop now, so she goes on, and she asks him, "What greater prize than your own dream?" The light of the pool dances on the bark of the pines and the leaves, which are light green and young and lively. She feels so excited to be here. "In return for their dreams I give them something they want more," says Full Lot Jack. "Something they crave, something they are longing for, whatever it might be."'

Takeru was silent now as well, listening to Em's story. She began to move through the trees, ducking behind and swaying against the trunks like a bird darting through mists.

'The girl feels, in her heart she knows, that this man means what he says. She looks at the pool again. So bright! It's heaven's light, captured on a forest floor. She says she'd like that, too.

What dreams does she have, anyway? A good husband? To see France? She says yes to the man with the puddle.'

A huge pine was lying fallen on the floor, its branches still covered with green needles. We climbed along its broken back, snapping at the twigs we could reach. 'How is that the end of the story?' asked Takeru. 'I mean, what's she actually getting? What's the deal meant to be? That story's just nonsense.' He sounded annoyed.

'It's a mystery,' said Em, her voice mocking. 'The girl wasn't the only one. There were others. Full Lot Jack always makes the same offer, in the end – every dream you own, in return for your heart's desire. That's the legend.'

'Where did you hear this stuff, really?'

'I told you, places. The heritage. I said.'

They frowned at each other.

'Are there any books, you know, about the myths?' I said. I jumped down from the broken back of the fallen pine. The ground was carpeted with needles, brown and dead and mouldering.

'Come on,' said Em, and she started to run off, heading out of the trees.

'Where to?' asked Takeru.

'You want to know all about the old stories?' she yelled. 'Then come on!'

'Where does she get all her energy from?' I muttered. Takeru shrugged, and we chased after her, off out of the woods and into the light.

We ran down through the grass fields, along the dirt path, back to the town where the earth became concrete, fences turned to walls, trees stood in lines with flowers planted neatly at the base. Em went ahead, laughing and singing to herself, and Takeru and I followed, obedient as toddlers. He scratched his head as we slowed to a walk. 'So . . .' I said, trying to think of what to say. 'So, Takeru's a cool name.'

'Thanks.'

'Where's it from?'

'It's Japanese. I already had it when I was adopted.'

'That's cool. Do you know Japanese?'

'Nah, I've never even been.'

I hoped I didn't sound annoying. He didn't seem to mind me quizzing him. We walked on.

'So you're here with your mum,' he said. It wasn't a question, wasn't quite a statement. We were trying to work each other out.

'I'm here with my mum,' I repeated, 'and my dad's coming later in the summer.'

In my head, clear and loud, I said, *liar*.

'He away on a trip?'

'Yeah,' I said. I stopped walking. I was glad I could talk, glad Mum wasn't here, or Rob, with smiles and busyness and silence. 'He's some sort of politician,' I said. Takeru had stopped beside me. 'He works for the government,' I went on, 'but here's the thing – no one'll tell me anything, but I know something happened and there's a mess, I think, that he has to help solve.'

'A mess?'

'I don't know,' I said. 'Something. Trouble. It's stupid.'

It's stories, I thought. *Stories and whispers.* I thought about Eren. Could I tell Takeru *that*? But I knew the answer. We started walking again.

'Bummer,' said Takeru. 'About your dad.' He tried to smile. 'What's he do?'

I shook my head. 'I asked once. Mum said it's something to do with money and how people get paid. He's cool, man, he has all these people to help him, and they have these awesome cars.'

'James Bond!' said Takeru. 'Hope I get to meet him. Think he'll take us for a ride?'

I laughed, but nothing was funny. Deep, deep down, I prayed. Let him come back soon, I thought, and we can all race together. Don't let anything be wrong.

We walked on. Em, at the corner of the road now, had stopped and turned back to us, hands on her hips, tapping her foot along to nothing but the sound of birdsong. 'Come *on*,' she said.

'Em, where are you taking us?'

'To see the lady who keeps the tales.'

'The lady,' repeated Takeru.

'The lady,' I said. Brilliant.

The road turned into a wider street, and at one of the houses, grand and red brick, we stopped. Em pointed to a tarnished gold sign on the wall. 'There,' she said with a firm nod. I read the sign out loud as Takeru looked up at the house and squinted in the sun.

'Coxborough Local History Society, est. 1925.'

'I told you, eh?' said Em. 'Let's see who's home!'

She pressed a small doorbell. It only took a few seconds for the door to open and a woman to step out. She was old, her white hair curled and thick, gold glasses hanging around her neck. She was thin, but not slow, and she smiled when she saw Em. 'Hello, stranger!' she said, and invited us inside.

'Hello, Mrs Barson. These are my friends. This is Takeru, he lives near me, and this is Oli – he's here with his mum for the summer.'

The lady, pink cardigan loose and soft, put on her glasses to see us. Takeru stood awkwardly. I tried to smile and settled for a nervous nod. She laughed gently, quietly. 'My, what handsome boys. I like that one's hair . . .' she said, and moved her hand towards Takeru. He muttered something and blushed.

'Nice to meet you, Mrs Barson,' I said.

'Please,' she said, 'call me Olive. Lovely to meet you, now.'

'Nice to meet you,' said Takeru, recovering and holding out his hand. Mrs Barson took it in both of hers, like a nun receiving a sinner, and then stood straighter. 'Well, young Em, what can I do for you today?'

'We were just up in the woods and I was telling them about Full Lot Jack.'

'Ohh, yes, yes,' she nodded.

'And I said you knew all about this place, and all its stories. You're the town's historian, I said.'

'Ha! Oh my,' said Mrs Barson, holding her hand to her chest in mock surprise. 'Such grandeur! I'm the current president

81

of the society, certainly, and I know a thing or two of the older stories.'

'May we look at your books?' asked Em.

Takeru leaned over to me again. 'Never knew she could be so polite,' he whispered.

Mrs Barson led us through to a sunny front room. I'd never seen one quite like it. Takeru let out a soft 'whoa!' as we took it all in. The walls were covered with photos, some black and white, some faded yellow, some framed, others stuck on corkboards. Shelves of books in material covers sat either side of the window, and cases with glass doors held rows of crazy things that didn't seem connected: brass watches, telescopes, stuffed animals – owls, voles – torn postcards, pottery, coins, silver knives, a sword, and a hundred other things I couldn't even name. In the centre was a table full of maps spread out ready to be studied. 'This place is awesome!' said Takeru as he moved around to stare at maps, charts, daggers, pots. I nodded and moved to the books. 'I'll get you kids some juice,' said Mrs Barson, walking out.

'Em, how'd you find this place?'

'It's not a secret, dimwit. It's a history society! My dad's actually a member.'

'What do they *do*?'

'Um . . . I don't know. Lots of this stuff has been collected just in case, in case someone wants it, or it's useful.'

'Mate, look at this, these are bullets!'

I moved over to see what Takeru was holding. They were round balls of clay, heavy and chipped. They felt cold. 'Stuff they found in the ground when they were building new houses,' said Em. The noise of glasses clinking echoed in the house. 'From the Civil War. Come on, let me show you some books about the woods,' she said, tugging our sleeves and taking us to a shelf across the room. *Local Legends*, it said in curly writing. *Coxborough, Morey Woods*. A few books were standing tightly together surrounded by leaflets and pamphlets – pages of stories, legends of ghosts, of churches, creatures, faeries, goblins, wolves and dark, winged things.

I thought about Eren. Goosebumps prickled my arms. I put the books down and stepped back again.

'Here you are,' said Mrs Barson, bringing in a tray of orange juice and biscuits. 'Now, anything particular I could help with? Nice to have people so interested in the society. Its heyday is long gone. Back in the forties and fifties, this place mattered more, to the locals. Back then there *were* locals, people whose families had lived here going back generations. Now people move here, or move away, and this place is more a museum.'

She walked over to see what Em and Takeru had found. 'Oh, *The Myths and Ghosts of Coxborough*,' she said, glancing at the book they were flicking through. 'Morey Woods used to be a great gathering place for the Little People, you know – goblins and faeries, sometimes a party of sprites. They've moved on now, but the echoes remain. You mentioned Full Lot Jack?'

'I was telling these guys the story in the woods,' said Em.

'Oh, calling up his name, no doubt? But he doesn't come any more. That shining pool of his is lost to mud.'

'Where did the story come from?' I asked. Mrs Barson ran her finger lightly along the books' spines and smiled.

'Where did it come from? From him, I suppose, originally; from Full Lot. But these tales get changed with every telling. Whenever a wanderer met him, they added their own truth to the fiction, no doubt.'

'How does the story end?' asked Takeru. He looked at Em and Mrs Barson with raised eyebrows, expectant.

The old woman chuckled again. 'You teasing the boys, Em? Letting your tales drag long and low?'

'I told them about the pool, the dreams, the offer, the price. It was the first girl.'

'Ah,' said Mrs Barson, 'the first girl to lose in that game. Come on, I'll tell the rest. Let me sit down, though. Drink your juice! Don't waste an old woman's effort.'

We took three chairs amongst the dust, the black eyes of a stuffed owl staring down from a shelf. I realised there were antlers perched on the wall above me.

'So the girl has been offered her desire, hmm?' asked Mrs Barson, and Em nodded, tucking her legs under her. *She's heard this all before*, I thought.

'Well then, let's keep going. The first record we have says that the girl agreed, all eager and bright, to give her dreams in exchange for a prize beyond her imagination. Full Lot Jack gets his name from the bargain he offers. She has to give him everything, willingly – the full lot of dreams she keeps stored up – and only then can Full Lot give her what she wants. She agrees. Now, depending on which version of the legend you have, at this point Full Lot either turns into a raven and flies away, or he turns into the pool of water himself, or he simply vanishes into the woods. The girl walks home, not saying a word to a soul, and settles into bed, and sleeps. The night passes, dark and silent, and she wakes, wondering only what her prize will be. She goes down to breakfast and greets her family – her mother, father and baby brother. They're staring at her, in a most uncomforting way. They look strange, she thinks. "What is it?" she asks. Her father speaks first. "Are you well, my love? You seem somewhat . . . pale."

'"You cannot be well!" says her mother. Her baby brother ignores her, even as she pats his head. "I'm quite all right, thank you," says she, and takes toast and eggs. Strange, though – the food seems so tasteless. She drinks tea. It gives her no pleasure. Perhaps she *is* ill, after all. She fetches a mirror, and her parents watch her, nervously, without turning their heads.

'Oh my!' Mrs Barson cried and brought her hands to her heart. Em giggled; Takeru and I watched, embarrassed, intrigued. 'Why, her eyes, they're near white! Her skin is pale, pale and feeling so cold. Her hair is flat and has no lustre, no sheen. She looks emptied.

'"That trickster!" she cries, but her voice has no power, no charge. What is she going to do? He has taken her dreams and her life and gone, fled away, with nothing to give back.'

Mrs Barson lowered her head to stare us right in the eyes.

'The girl searches for him, and tries to find help in others, but none will believe her – her words always sound so false, so fluttering and wispy, smoke caught on a breeze, butterflies flapping on windows, nothing to stir people to move. She wanders in the woods, looking for light, looking for Full Lot, but of course he is not there. She has sold her dreams for nothing but hot air and tricks. A lost cause.'

Em clapped suddenly, making us jump. 'You see, you should respect the woods! Don't ever sell your dreams, eh?'

'Indeed, Emma. Full Lot's a clever one. He knows where each of us is weakest,' said Mrs Barson.

'And that's a local thing, is it?' asked Takeru.

Mrs Barson smiled. 'All recorded here, dear,' she said, picking up a book from a nearby shelf. *Tales and Hauntings of Morey*, cheap, faded and thin.

'Thank you,' I said, 'that was really interesting.'

'Oh, the stories with soul in them always are. Give me a mystery from a wood of my own over aliens and gunfire any day.'

We thanked her again and started for the front door. The house's silence seemed heavy. We shuffled out, none of us talking. When I was in the doorway, I felt a hand rest lightly on my shoulder. I turned around.

'Take care, dear,' said Mrs Barson.

'Um,' I said. 'Sure.' Em and Takeru were already outside, waiting.

'If you ever need to chat . . . I know it's not easy being new in town,' she said. 'And things are hard, I'm sure.'

I frowned. 'Sorry?'

She blinked, and nodded without saying anything. 'Not my place,' she said. 'You run along.'

She lowered her gold glasses again and let them fall loose on the chain, standing in the doorway as I walked back out to the street. Em cocked her head. I shrugged. 'Just saying goodbye,' I said.

⚜

We headed home. The sun was high and we were hungry.

'She's pretty cool, right?' asked Em. Takeru and I nodded. 'We can go back there another time. Give the society something to do.'

'Give *her* something to do, you mean!'

'Same thing,' said Em.

I said goodbye to them outside Takeru's house and walked around to Uncle Rob's. I had to go back to the loft. I had to.

I had to see Eren.

ELEVEN

'We are the dreamers of dreams,' he says. 'Magic. Wow. Magic. What a lady. I should so like to get to know her.'

'Mrs Barson?'

'You paint a fine picture of her, my boy. A fine, fine picture. A book keeper! Gods of the word, they are. Finest of the brave. You know, it's them that keep books,' he says, 'that know things, in the end.'

He turns away from me and stares into blackness and shadows. 'No greater fear or happiness,' he whispers, 'than for those who keep the books alive.'

⁂

I SNUCK IN the house, making sure no one saw me. Mum was in the kitchen, arguing on the phone. I stopped for a second to listen for Dad's name, but whoever she was shouting at, it didn't seem like someone I knew. The sound of rustling bags and clinking plates followed me upstairs. The loft ladder pulled down easier than before – it was getting less stuck every time. I paused, breathing heavily for just a second, watching the pale leaves outside my window. I put my foot on the bottom rung and climbed. As my head bobbed into the gloom I saw a shape move in the shadows near the window.

'You again,' he said in a hoarse whisper. He groaned and coughed. 'Twice in a day, I'm a lucky one, eh? Come to finish the story?'

'Eren,' I said. It was the most powerful word I could think of. It meant everything.

He bowed and hobbled over and grinned like a devil. 'Three pigs,' he said, 'and only two houses gone. It's time for me pudding. Away we go!'

That was what he wanted, before anything else? It seemed like so little.

'The third house was made of bricks,' I said, and he nodded along with his eyes closed, swaying his head, a monster in prayer. 'The wolf came, and he huffed, and puffed, but the bricks were strong, the cement was dry and solid, and no matter how hard he blew, nothing happened.'

'He should try harder,' said Eren. 'Everyone falls in the end. He should blow into their weak spot.'

'Uh . . . he does, he blows harder, but you can't blow over a house made of bricks.'

'*You* can't blow over a house made of bricks, you mean.' He licks his lips and pats his rough furred belly.

'The wolf stops, and thinks. The door is locked, the windows tight closed – how can he get in? He's hungry, after so much huffing and puffing.'

'And effin' and blindin', I'm sure,' said Eren. He opened his eyes and smiled at me. 'Go on, then, go on, let me hear it all!'

'The wolf climbed the house! He had seen, on the roof . . .'

I paused for a moment, '. . . a chimney!'

'Oh, heavens! Oh, vengeance!'

I'd started to enjoy telling the story, I realised. I was enjoying 'The Three Little Pigs'. Eren leaned towards me, desperate to hear what I said next. I had the power of the storyteller. I felt slightly odd. His breath – Eren's breath – touched the hairs on my head and moved them slightly. He moved back and I stared at him. 'The pigs aren't stupid, though – not the third one, anyway. He sees the wolf's plan, he knows what will happen if the beast gets inside.'

'Never let the beast in, that's for sure.'

'"Quick, quick!" he tells his brothers. "He'll come down the chimney, but why don't we let him? Let him come all the way . . . to the pot! We can boil him, smash him, get rid of him for good!" They all agree, and the trap is set. The fire is lit, the water is heating, the pot is hot iron, hissing and steaming away. On the roof they hear the scratches of beasty claws.'

In my mind I heard the tapping of nail on slate, felt my skin prickle as the wolf's howl echoed, watched the steam rise and spit in the boiling iron pot. Eren was moving closer again, hanging on my words. I had the power here.

'Then, with a crash, the house is shaking. The chimney fills with dust as the wolf tears down it, ready to get three pork rolls in his belly. Splash! The pot rattles and chimes, the wolf howls, thrashes around, the pigs fall back in terror, squealing and snorting, sparks fly, iron sings out as the wolf bites down, and then . . . and then . . . !'

I was throwing my arms around, lost in the moment. I felt

dizzy, spun out of control; the story was spilling over, bubbling around its mould, becoming wild and dangerous and raw. As I moved recklessly around, crying out the words, I caught sight of Eren. He was laughing as he watched me, mouthing along to my story. I stumbled, fell over, and the silence in the attic was so heavy I thought it might drown me. Time held its breath.

'He dies,' said Eren in a tiny, far-off whisper. 'The wolf has lost, and the pigs, the victors, shall always be remembered. Thank you, Oli.'

I was sweating, panting, my eyes were stinging. Eren moved away to stare out of the window, turning his back to me and holding his hands together.

'I—' I said, but he shushed me without turning around.

'You are special,' he said. 'That's all. You have a flair for this kind of thing. You will be fine. I'm tired now, but thankful. Maybe you'd best be off, eh?'

'What are you?' I asked again. Had I really seen his lips moving with mine? Had I imagined it?

'That sounds an easy question,' he said, 'but that's only 'cause of what *you* are. Be happy, for now, knowing that I'm here, knowing what I ain't. I ain't many things.'

'Tell me more. About you,' I said. I felt like the first man to meet an alien, an angel, a dinosaur. How could I not ask for more?

He snorted at my question and waved his hand around the room. 'Look at this! Dust and shadows and forgotten things. Nothing to live on here. But I waited, didn't I?'

'What for?'

'Someone up to the task.'

'Me?'

'You're proving an ingenious little bugger, aye.'

'Tell me more, Eren!'

'Oh, that name,' he said, holding his head, chuckling low and dark. *Like a bear*, I thought. 'I'll tell you more,' he said. 'Hell's words, I'll show you more, mark it. You in for more, Oli?'

What was he offering? I thought of Mum, Bekah, Uncle Rob and Dad.

'Yes. Show me,' I said.

In the dust a fly buzzed and jerked through the air, lost and drunk and dying. Eren moved slowly, in shuffles and steps that creaked, tattered wings rustling behind him with a sound like dry leaves and fire. As he stepped nearer, the light from the window behind him threw his shadow against my face and I felt the cold rising.

'I will touch you between your eyes,' he said. A single digit stretched towards me and I held my breath. His eyes, black and deep, shone even then. His touch was dry and faint and weak, like the touch of a silk scarf lightly tapping my skin. 'Now,' he said, 'let's go back.'

Deep in my stomach something lurched, and I felt myself spinning out of the loft.

❦

Me and him, me and Eren, were crouching low behind rocks, staring out at the patchy grass. The sky was baking in the high sun, and an entire plain spread out before us – light-yellow grasses, boulders and rocks jutting harshly through, a river winding lazily to the horizon.

'My memories,' said Eren. He looked like a moulting vulture, or a crow, black and hazy but jagged, too. 'My youth.'

I heard voices from behind a high stone and moved around to see. 'They can't see you,' said Eren. 'This all happened a long time ago. Years and years, like you couldn't imagine.'

'What year is it?'

'No years. Not invented yet. No countries yet. Nothing but man and the things he knows.'

Three men were sitting on the ground, cooking meat over a fire. Their hair was tangled and long, they all had thick beards, and clothes made from animal fur and nothing more. The meat hung on a stick, juicy and spitting and sweet. 'Who are they?' I asked.

'They're no one special. Nothing much to do. But they're some of the first.'

'First?'

'Hell, I remember all of this. So long ago, a time you can't imagine.'

The men sat in silence, chewing on gristle, staring off at the open world, or watching the sun cross the sky. Then, suddenly, one of them spoke. He spoke in a strange, choking way, harsh but soft. He kept stopping, letting his words hang in the air before starting up again. The two other men watched him, or listened – I couldn't tell.

'He is telling them about a beast he has heard of,' said Eren. 'A beast he has seen.'

'Seen?'

'Heard of.'

'Which?' I asked, staring at the man again. His dark eyes squinted in the sun as he spoke.

'Both. Neither. It's not the same as it will be, later. They don't really mark the difference.'

The man was moving his hands in time to his words, showing sizes, mimicking animals, and once or twice he hooted and chuckled. His friends watched and waited.

'He's telling them about the beast, about its size, its ferocity, its anger. No one could ever kill it. It will kill everything else, he says. Watch, watch what he does now . . .'

The man continued speaking and leaned forward to turn the meat. It hissed and the fat dripped into the flames. Eren sighed. 'He is imagining, out loud, where the beast might live, and is wondering, to himself, what kind of man would tame it.'

'He's imagining?'

'He is creating, boy. Creating a story that will later be told to others by both these men, listening now, as if it were theirs. When they tell it the hunter will kill the beast, or the beast will kill the hunter and devour him piece by piece. Different versions, spreading over the grass and the dust. He,' says Eren, pointing, 'he is the first teller, though.'

I moved closer. The men didn't see me, didn't move at all. The storyteller's audience were ensorcelled. Their eyes, dark and deep-set, opened wide in amazement as the man continued talking, and when he stopped, they both gazed deep into the fire, and stretched their necks back to stare at the sky.

'These men, their families, their language, their tales, their memories will die out long before a person ever even holds a pen. This world will pass into nothing before *your* people even know what metal is.'

I stared at the sun, high and yellow, righter and whiter than I had seen it. It was something ancient. I felt its power. Eren sighed and turned to me, his black shape filling my mind. 'And from this I came, like the fire that bursts from the green trees, the wave that bubbles from the oceans. Stories were told, and they had power, and I was born, always hungry, always thirsty, seeking more, keeping the balance. That's all you can know,' he said. 'I am something that came after, and I was fed well.'

'You're old,' I said, not meaning it as a question, not wanting him to agree with me. He touched me, once, between my eyes, and the old, lost world faded into sand and wind, and I felt the attic floor beneath my feet. He shuffled away and said, over one shoulder, 'Next . . . next time – when I am stronger again – you will share your own story with me. Just a slice, what do you say? A nice, juicy bit of Oli's life, for a poor old thing like me.'

'What?'

'I showed you a part of me, and now I want a part of you. Three pigs is good – it's a snack – but it's not *your* tale, is it? Fair's fair, little warrior. I want to hear about you. You're so interesting. You're so special. Next time, eh?'

I nodded and climbed down the ladder, feeling small and tired. The sound of Mum in the kitchen surprised me with its blandness. The ring of dead wind still rumbled and echoed in my ears.

TWELVE

Eren gives me a strange look, an unreadable mixture of loss and something else.

'You won't have understood all that,' he says. I agree, sitting before him. I'm only just beginning to understand. Little pieces, bit by bit, drips and drops. He sighs and laughs.

'You're here now, so you can begin to see. There are things beyond the places you have been.'

'It was . . . ancient,' I say. The word is right, the only word I can think of that approaches that place.

'It was a beginning,' he says. 'Do you know the ending?'

Is this a test, then? Maybe I can survive him. It's a warm thought.

'There is no end,' I say, and the sound of him clapping explodes through my mind.

'Bravo! "There is no end," he says.' He swoops down and his wings darken my sky. 'No end, Oli. Tales go on and on. They come from before you were born, and they echo on after you leave.'

'HEY, THERE you are!' said Mum. She looked annoyed. 'Oli, come on, help unpack the shopping.' She pulled a loaf of bread out of a bag and thumped it down heavily on the table.

I felt tired and empty. My stomach hurt. 'What's up?' I asked. The wrinkles around her eyes were more obvious than normal. She held herself stooped over the sink, looking like a frightened child.

'I'm fine, Oli, just busy, and I'd appreciate the help.'

'Sure. Sorry, Mum.'

I took cans and fruit out of plastic bags and did my best to find where they could go. Mum stayed at the sink, her hands gripping the edge, breathing deeply and staring into nothing.

'Bad news about your dad, Oli,' she said suddenly. My stomach turned cold and I turned to look at her. She had her eyes closed as if she were remembering a song. 'He's going to stay in London for a bit.'

'I thought he was coming soon?'

'No. No, he's staying down.'

'Why?'

'There are . . . problems at work. You know your dad has a very important job.'

'He works for the government,' I said.

'Yes,' said Mum slowly. 'Yes, he does. And there are some hard times at the moment, so he's . . . staying, to try to work things out.'

'He's not coming here, then?'

'No. No, he can't.'

'For how long?'

'I don't know, Oli!' she shouted. She gasped and stopped herself. 'Oh, darling, I'm sorry. It's just difficult. It's . . . a big, big problem. But nothing he can't handle, I'm sure. You know your father—'

'It's OK, Mum, really. I don't mind it here. I really don't. We can stay for the summer. It's OK.'

'Yes, I think we should,' she said. 'We should have come here long ago.'

'Uncle Rob said he's been to London before.'

She gave a tiny laugh. 'Oh, yes. But it's been years, now. Ages. Your father and Rob don't really see eye to eye on a lot of things, which made it hard.'

I put away the cheese she'd bought, and the ham and the juice.

'Rob was a proper trouble maker, back in the day,' said Mum. 'He always meant to be, too. Gave your dad some headaches back when we still lived here, when he was working on more local projects. Just planning approval, things like that, but . . .' She stopped and looked up out of the window. 'Before we moved to London, all this. Before your dad climbed the ranks,' she said.

'So you moved.'

'And Rob stayed, yes.'

'Why would they argue?' I asked.

'Ha!' she said bitterly. 'They're both a bit proud. Your uncle just doesn't really agree with a lot of what your dad does. They're . . . very different men, Oli. Both like to have their own way. But they're both good in their hearts. You know Rob once chained himself to a tree?' she said, starting to laugh.

'A *tree*? Why?'

'It was to stop the trees being chopped down and the land being cleared. Oh, he was so proud of himself for doing that. My goodness, I haven't thought about that for years. You have to ask him about it. Oh! And the time he and some of his friends were so angry about the pollution of a reservoir, they took a whole fleet of canoes and launched a furious little armada onto the water. I bet I still have pictures. He was so young!'

'Dad and Rob, they both love you, though,' I said.

She looked at me, nodded, and didn't say anything.

'We'll stay here for a bit,' I said, putting my hand on her shoulder. 'Dad can come when he's finished. He has to come. I want him to meet Takeru.'

Mum sighed.

'OK,' I said. I moved back to the shopping.

⚜

Em was lying on the grass, pulling at daisies without opening her eyes. I lay next to her, Takeru beside me, staring at the clouds, and at nothing.

'She's pretty cool,' he said. 'But that stuff, it's kind of weird.'

'The society,' I said. We all murmured.

'It's a cool story though, right?' asked Em.

We all waited in silence for a minute. The clouds above didn't seem to be any particular shape to me – just swirls of white and froth.

'You said there are more stories about Coxborough and Morey Wood?' I said.

'Yeah.'

Takeru nudged me and rolled his eyes. 'You read them all, Em?'

She tutted. The sky slipped along above us and we lay without talking, not caring about the time. Nobody spoke, nothing happened. I closed my eyes and felt myself float away. The grass was cold, the sound of the town dim and throbbing. I could feel myself tumble inside my own head, the heat of the sun on my face suddenly foreign and strange. Like falling asleep and then jerking awake. I knew that I wasn't alone in the field but the world seemed suddenly heavy, suddenly too *thick*. I let colours flash behind my closed eyes, and imagined stars where I couldn't see them. The wind blew grass seeds against my face and I twitched a finger, reminding myself where I really was.

'You are many places!' screamed a sudden, dust-dry voice inside my ear, too close and too real to be a memory.

I gave a shout of surprise and sat up. Takeru and Em both sat up too, smirking. 'Bug?' asked Em.

'Maybe a . . . maybe a beetle,' I said.

'A bug! A creepy-crawly, am I?' whispered the voice, brittle as old bone.

'They won't hurt you,' said Takeru, lying down again on the grass.

I rubbed my ear and looked around. He was here. I knew he was. I closed my eyes again and felt my heart beat in my chest.

'Boom, boom!' said the voice, as faint as the wings of a moth. *'Belief isn't everything.'*

I stood up. He *was* here. Could he move around?

'Eren,' I mouthed at the sky. Em and Takeru stood up too, watching, bemused, as I rubbed my head.

'You really hate creepy-crawlies, eh?'

They kept laughing and tearing up pieces of grass to tickle each other's ears with. I tried to look relaxed. He was *with* me.

I gritted my teeth.

'Listen,' said Em, 'you want to come to mine? We can pick some apples.'

'Sweet!' said Takeru enthusiastically.

'Up for it, Oli?'

'Huh?'

'Picking apples?' she said.

The field was empty, the sky still light and clear. He couldn't be here.

'Uh, yeah, let's go,' I said. 'I mean, that sounds good.'

'Let's go through the Portal,' said Takeru. He raised his arms up and did a bad impression of a ghost, letting the word drag on as he hooted. 'The Poooortaaaaal!'

'The Portal!' laughed Em. 'I haven't called it that for a while. It's the secret gate we used, Oli.'

'A *secret* portal!' said Takeru dramatically. 'Actually, I think secret portals should lead to cooler things than apples.'

Em thumped him on the arm and he moved away, running down the field.

'What's a good thing for a portal to lead to?' he called over his shoulder.

'New worlds!' cried Em. 'Dream lands. The past!'

'Monsters,' I said, running after him.

We ran madly, wildly, back down into town, dodging between parked cars and shrieking like loons. Cats joined us as we tore down the road and threw ourselves into the alley beside Takeru's house. At the end of his garden we stopped, and Em cast a searching glance back at the house. 'Parents aren't in, are they?' she asked.

'We're clear, don't worry.'

Takeru led us through the bushes until we found the fence and the thin, almost invisible line that marked the Portal. 'Got to pull it from this side,' he said, and pushed two fingers into the soil beneath it, feeling for the door until he felt it give, and a space opened up.

'Into the magic!' said Em as she pushed through into her own garden. I followed, brushing cobwebs away from my face, and Takeru came last, letting the door fall neatly back into place.

'Amazing, eh?' he said, turning to me.

'Best portal I've ever been through,' I said.

'Ha!'

Em led us into the orchard. The trees, bent and twisted, seemed almost dragged down by the apples covering the branches. My eyes flicked up to the attic window of Uncle Rob's house. I knew, I *knew*, he was in there.

'Eren, the watcher,' I said under my breath. It seemed right. 'Eren, the waiter.'

'What's that?' asked Takeru.

'Nothing.'

102

'The crow's gone,' said Em. 'The dead one. Dad got rid of it. Said it'd attract cats. I said, so what? Cats are great!'

'I like dogs,' said Takeru.

'Cats,' said Em, in a whisper to me like she was sharing a secret, 'are where the real magic lies. What are dogs? They're just pets. Cats are noble.'

'Wolves are noble,' said Takeru. 'They're hunters, they're prowlers, all teeth and fangs and a sudden red spurt in the night! Cats are just pillows.'

'Cats are whispers and silk. Help us out here, Oli?' said Em.

'Oli?' said Takeru.

They both stared at me, waiting for me to settle the argument, but the only eyes I could feel were his. He was there.

'Bats,' I said.

Em frowned. 'Eh?'

'Bats are night-time. They're velvet dark and diamond light. Bats are . . . they're glistening dew on dark lakes. Bats fly and crawl, burrow and hang. They feed.'

'Never seen a bat,' said Takeru. 'You make them sound . . . strange.'

I shrugged. I didn't know. 'There you go. We picking apples, then?'

Em rushed inside. I could hear her banging and clattering through cupboards. I looked up at the trees. The apples didn't look that great – they were yellowed, marked, strangely shaped, some eaten by worms, some browning as they grew.

'Believe me, they make a good pie,' said Takeru.

Em came back with three bowls and two long poles –

103

broom handles with the heads cut off. 'Whack and catch!' she explained as she saw my puzzled face. 'You can't climb up these branches too far – they're old, and they'd just snap off. So, to get the apples before they actually just fall and splatter in the grass for the worms and the crawly-creeps, we give them a gentle bash.'

'If you hit them too hard they just splatter in mid-air!' said Takeru. 'Covers the catcher with apple sauce.'

'Apples go best in pies, *not* hair. So, you beat – *lightly* – and I will catch. And if you want,' she said, fixing Takeru with a cold stare, 'I *can* tell you another story from that book. A story that just *happens* to have apples in it.'

'You set all this up!' said Takeru.

'Bash the apples, Tak, or I bash you.'

'I want to hear it, Em,' I said, trying to keep my voice calm. 'Tell us the story.'

'Well, all right, then.'

She handed me a pole, and Takeru another, and stood underneath holding the largest bowl. 'Ready?' she asked. 'Go!'

I lifted the stick up to pat the apple nearest me, and Em began her story.

THIRTEEN

'Look out of the window,' he says. I look. The forest, the road, the sky, the moon. All hazy and far away. 'Could you tell me what they look like, in such detail, in such vivid colour that I could paint them, and not be a hair off reality?'

'What? No . . . how could I ever remember . . . ?'

'Could you tell me what your face looks like? You've had it long enough, ugly mug that it is! How big is your nose, how far from your mouth?'

'I don't get—'

'I know you don't, puddle,' he says. 'Is it this hard for you people? Details ain't what matter. I tell you there's a moon, you imagine a moon. You make up the way it looks 'cause you know what a moon looks like.'

'Telling a story – hearing a story – is like making up your own . . . ?' I say. He nods for a moment, then points out the window again. A grey cloud spreading over a grey sky.

'That's all yours,' he says. 'You made it, even if you can't tell me right now what a moon flippin' looks like.'

'I didn't make this, Eren, we're—'

'Where are we?' His voice is hard, a knife cutting

through the darkness and the cold.

'We're in the loft,' I say.

'Then tell me this, if we really are still there: how many panes of glass make up that window?'

Turning, I frown and start to count. One, two, three, then across the top and . . . No. I must have stopped paying attention. One, two, then at the side there are one, two, four and then . . . my eyes are slipping away from the corners. I can't focus on how many edges the window has. I try to force myself to touch them one by one, but it seems so impossible, so ridiculous. I can't see where the window starts and stops.

'We left this place a while back,' says Eren, putting a hand on my shoulder. I shiver. 'You've done a good job on making this new 'un, this new world, but you're trying to count something that isn't there, boy. Whispers and dreams and shows. Nothing here is real, any more, nothing here is solid and countable. Do you know where we are, boy?'

I can't believe him. I try to run, away from him, away from here, down to the house, but the floor, grey and bare, isn't moving even though I'm running. The window behind me is throwing dead light into the corners of the room, so near, so far away, and then gone. I can't leave.

'What is this?' I shout. A flutter of wings and shadow move in the space in front of me and Eren is standing over me, wrapped in velvet and silence.

'You know where we is, boy!' he says, a high laugh

curling his lips. 'We're in your story, now.'

We're in your story, now.

He's in my story.

It's all a story.

How long have I been here?

❧

'ONCE UPON a time,' said Em, 'there was a moonlit orchard. Not this one, but one nearby – the field is still there, but the trees are all gone. This is the story of what happened. There was an orchard, and it was doing well – they made cider every year, really good stuff, fruity and dark, enough to make all the people's heads spin. The farmer – he's long since dead – was growing rich and happy with that land. But one night something happened to change the fate of that place. The moon was a slim twist of white in the sky, no more than a slice of light you could barely see. The stars were flashing and dancing, and then – whoosh! – something fiery and huge fell down, scorching the ground where it lay, cooking all the apples on the trees nearest it, turning the grass black and the soil to clay. A fallen star! Silver lightning crackled in the air and golden dust fell like rain. The orchard was silent, and then . . .

'"What's this, what's this?" said a voice in the gloom. The farmer? No, he was in bed. A stranger? Not in this place. It was someone older. It was the apple-lord, woken from his sleep by the shudder of the fall. The fallen star was something *real*, you see, the first real thing to happen in a while, enough to wake

107

him up more than any storm or party or machine made by men could. He was shaken awake!'

Takeru and I listened, glancing at each other as we tried to reach the higher branches. An apple fell onto the ground beside Em with a gentle thud, and she stooped to pick it up before going on.

"'What's this? What's this?" he asked in his old, woody voice, and he walked towards the cindering hole. He looked like an old man, all ruddy and healthy, an autumn man, with a fiery red beard and deep, piercing eyes.

"'Help me,' said a tiny, silvery voice. The apple-lord leaned forward to see what was talking.

"'Who asks help of the orchard?' he asked, booming and bellowing.

"'Help me,' said the tiny voice again. He peered in, and gasped, surprised to see something far wilder than all his deepest dreams. The fallen star, a tiny boy, looked up at him and reached out his arms. "Help!" said the boy-star. "I'm lost!"

"'I should think so,' said the apple-lord. "You're on earth, in my orchard, and you've woken me by your falling! You should be up in the night sky, son."

"'I fell from my mother's ship, as I leaned over to see the earth-beneath-the-water."

"'Not water, but the sky itself,' said the apple-lord. The star, the boy, shone silver and white in the dark soil and looked up at him.

"'What can I do?' he asked. "How do you get back up?"

'Now, apple-lords are Kings of Trees, and their reach is only as high as their branches. The apple-lord knew nothing about the sky, and nothing about the night – his power reached only to the edge of the orchard. Beyond that, even earth and soil weren't his to command. He sighed a big, woody sigh. "I can't help you, little star," he said. "I have no power to do so."

'The boy-star sucked at his fingers and looked into the ancient eyes of the apple-lord. "Bring me a cat," he said. "Can you do that? I was always told to ask a cat for help, if I fell."'

As Em told the story she moved the bowl from side to side and walked around the tree, catching the fruit we knocked down. I knew that Eren would hear what she said. I hit the apple branches a little harder.

'The apple-lord searched through his orchard, from fence to fence, from root to leaves, and found a cat to call. On padded feet as silent as a grave, it came to his side and waited. "This boy is a fallen star," said the apple-lord, "and he asked to speak to you. He wants to return home."

'The cat flicked its head sideways and whipped its tail in the grass. "Indeed?" it asked, ever so silkily.

'"You're in the orchard," said the lord, "and you have to respect that. I command you to help him."

'"I was sleeping under a tree, resting, so I could hunt for mice later," said the cat, "and I didn't agree to this."

'But the cat knew he was stuck. He knew it was true – the orchard was the apple-lord's world, and if he slept there, he was his servant. What bad luck to be here on the night the star fell and the king woke up! The cat jumped down to the boy.

'"What do you want, star-child?" he asked, angrily. Cats are clever and proud and independent, and he was insulted by the apple-lord's words, no matter how right they were.

'"I fell," said the boy-star. "I fell from my mother's boat above the clouds and above the sky. I was told, though, that being a cat, you might know a way back – I was always told, ask the cats, they know things."

'The cat purred and whipped his tail. "Yes, oh yes, we do."

'The apple-lord looked down on them, down there in the hole. "Is there a way? I can't have a star smouldering in the orchard, even a baby one! Look at the trees, look at the fruit, they're burned and dead already!"

'"I can get you home," said the cat. "It's something I know all about."

'Imagine how happy the star was! He laughed and thanked the cat, and it purred but stared daggers at the apple-lord. The cat leaned close to the star and whispered over to him, ever so smoothly, so that no one else could hear. The cat told the secret of how to return to the sky, how to fly up and up and then splash out to the surface of the stars, and not to fall back down. The apple-lord watched the star's face twist in surprise, and shock, and joy, and happiness. He saw the cat's tail swish, swish, swish and felt uneasy. *Something*, he thought, *is coming*.'

'Let's move on to the next tree,' said Takeru. 'This one's almost done.'

'Yeah, leave the highest fruit for now,' said Em. 'Start again at the low ones. They'll come off easy, one hit.'

I tapped on the yellow leaves and an apple fell into the bowl.

Em smiled and went on.

'The cat wandered off, and left the orchard that night. The star-boy was silent, staring at the lord with empty, shining eyes. Hours passed – it looked like morning would come before the star would do anything. "Well," said the apple-lord, "I will sleep, even if you won't. I have given you help, and allowed your trespass into the orchard. That much is over – you're on your own, I fear!"

'He slept, then, the deep, natural sleep of the Tree Kings, a long sleep, one that would not normally end for many years. As the apple-lord slept, the star-boy stood, and went to work, carrying out the cat's words. Do you know what he did?'

'No,' I said, and Takeru shook his head, our poles hovering in mid-air.

'He did what the cat said – and cut off every apple from every tree, slicing them neatly in half, the top from the bottom, and peering inside. What did he see?'

The darkness of the attic window twitched like an evening shadow.

'What?' said Takeru.

'*Stars*,' said Em. 'An apple cut in half'll show a star – and an orchard cut in half will show a sky full of them. The more apple-stars he saw, the stronger the star-boy felt. And the stronger he felt the brighter he shone – brighter and brighter until he thought he could see his mother, far above. He waved, and she reached down to take him. The orchard was silent, empty, and broken – not a single apple left.

'The apple-lord awoke, roused by the change he felt even in

111

the depths of his dreams. He looked out over his trees and felt their empty deaths deep down to his roots. "You killed me," he said to the cat, who had slunk back between the posts of the fence, sniffing at the broken leaves. His voice was calm, but surprised. Death was something he understood, something that was part of Nature, part of him, but still . . . perhaps he was hurt, even.

"'I have,' said the cat, "but my words were true – the star is gone."

"'Was that the only way?'"

"'That he should see every star in every apple? No,' said the cat. "No, it wasn't.'"

"'I offended you.'"

"'Know better, next time, apple-lord, before you meddle with a cat.'"

"'No,' said the king with the voice of wind through the branches, "there is no next time. The orchard is dead.'"

"'There'll be mice in the empty trunks.'"

"'I can't feel sorry for that,' said the apple-lord, in a voice like the rustle of dead leaves. The stars overhead blinked out as the morning sun rose.'

Em gave a tiny bow and curtseyed, holding the hem of an invisible skirt. 'The end!' she said, nodding happily and putting down the bowl. Takeru and I threw the poles to the ground and picked up the last few apples from the ground.

'That whole story just because an orchard died?' Takeru asked.

'Apparently they really found all the apples one day, cut up and showing their stars. I think they thought it was a curse, and burned the trees. Imagine! The old apple-lord burning in the copper flames, red-specked beard all crispy and smoking in autumn . . .'

Takeru laughed. 'Seriously, though, you're good at telling the stories. You should be an actor.'

Em blushed and smiled. 'No, no . . . but it's fun. You should try it. I bet you could think of a great one!'

'I think . . .' I said, louder than I meant to, 'I think we should do something with these apples. Now, yeah?'

'Em, I think you spooked Oli,' said Takeru.

'Whatever,' I said, trying to keep my voice cool. I was desperate to get inside, away from the glare, to silence the thoughts that bounced and echoed round my head. *Eren's here, he listens, he hears, the stories . . .*

The attic window glistened in the sunlight.

FOURTEEN

I watch him as he sits in the twilight, his eyes shut fast, his breathing shallow. He's humming to himself, or to me, or to nobody. Maybe he isn't really humming. I look around at where we are, but my focus slips from the corners as if they were black ice. I squint but I can't see. Eren sits and hums, or dreams. I move around, feeling out for the edges of the attic, moving towards the window that watches the world. It's just too far. Just a little beyond my reach . . .

This room isn't a room. I can't work it out. And then Eren is standing next to me, his eyes like tiny suns floating in black water.

'It's more of a thought,' he says, 'than any room you would recognise.'

THERE WERE birds flying overhead. They looked like nothing more than scratches in the sky, but I heard their cries, wild and crazed, shattering the silence of the open fields. I was running through the empty spaces of a lost world. A hungry sun blazed fiercely in the sky. Shadows passed under my feet, dark smears and stains on the ground around me. I called out to Eren. I ran until I heard waves crashing and then saw an ocean of grey, hard water open up in front of me, filling in from rivers on all sides.

'Eren!' I shouted, scrabbling down the shingle onto the beach. All stones, white and black and fist-sized. No sand yet – that would come later. The sun fizzed like the static on television and crackled into darkness. A thousand stars fell from the sky, turning the beach white and milky with fog. There was a boy ahead of me. 'I cannot find my way,' he said, but I pushed past him, chasing the black haze that darted and ran ahead of me. 'Eren, wait!'

Why was Eren running away? I had to tell him something. Something too important to wait. From the sea a sad, silent woman stepped up and danced with the stars, her wet black eyes searching their twinkling faces.

'I search for a king!' she cried as she spun and twirled.

From the distant forest a cat's meow rippled like laughter. 'The kings have gone to the stars!' it purred. 'The stars have gone to the dogs!'

I ran on, following Eren, reaching out for him. There was nothing but burnt orange earth under my feet now, my soles clapping and cracking as I pounded on. High above me, the birds soared and span.

'Eren . . . *stop*!' I shouted.

He did, finally, skidding to a halt, his blur turning solid, his wings, his snout, his eyes, merry, hungry.

'Who commands me like that?' he asked. I walked forward.

The dull, young earth spat dust onto my trainers.

'Eren,' I said.

'Ahh,' he said, as if he'd suddenly understood something, something he hadn't even thought about. 'Oli. So we're meeting here too, now.'

'Eren, I've got something to tell you.'

'Oh yes? Hmm?' He raised a cynical eyebrow. His sharp pointed teeth hung over his lips when he smiled.

'I . . .' Why was it so hard to remember? I was sure there was something . . . something vague and slippery. My mind wouldn't focus.

'In dreams there are very rarely answers,' he said, 'but you can't really be surprised. It's not what they're for. Questions, now *that's* what you get from dreams. Questions and . . . how can I put this? Hints.'

'Hints?' The sound of the waves was coming nearer. I turned and saw the ocean pushing over the beach, racing over the parched land.

'Cheats,' he said. 'Dreams are where . . . where advice can be given, if things are right. But you had something to *tell* me?'

'No, I guess – no – I just saw you and—'

'Wake up, Oli.'

'What?'

'Wake up! And look out of the window when you do.'

⁂

I sat up with a grunt, staring around, trying to see. Darkness hung like a fog in my room, and I reached out groggily for

117

my clock. 12:16. My eyes were still half closed, but I turned around and groped at the curtain with an arm as heavy as lead, my skin sensing the rush of cold off the glass like a tiny sting. I mumbled to myself, nothing in particular, and pulled myself up to sitting. The warmth of my bed called me back, but I sighed deeply, cleared my throat, and reached forward to rub mist from the glass. What was I looking for?

I gasped. In the high branches of the tree outside, a dark-grey cat was staring at me, his fur glowing almost purple in the gloom. He nodded, blinked, and flicked his tail. I stared at him as he nodded again and pawed the air between us.

'Open the window?' I asked. Stupid, I told myself, talking to a cat, but . . . the cat bowed its head again, nodding once. *Yes.* The window was an old one, and slid up instead of swinging out, but I managed it quickly enough. The cat licked its paw and the pinkness of its tongue was like a splash of blood in the dark tree's branches.

'It was not as hateful as it seemed,' it said, in a voice that rasped like a grandfather's. I froze, wide-eyed and shivering.

'Oh, don't look at me like that, puh-*lease*. Insults are insults – it's one of the basic laws, the *rules* of things like us.'

'Us?' I managed to croak. I rubbed my eyes, looked at my clock. 12:18. The wind rustled the curtains and brushed my neck. I was awake, at least.

'Old things. Natural things. Real things. That fruity lord – the apple guy – him, too. Me. Us all.'

'You're . . . from the orchard?'

'I must say, I thought you'd be faster than this. I was told you were *inspiring*. The exact words. Yes, I am the same. And as I said, there are rules, for our kind. Insults are insults, and are heavy, serious things. It's like . . . blood for blood. Bowing to the orders of boundaries. Don't cross water to catch your prey. Rules,' said the cat.

'The story, that was *you*,' I said.

His eyes flashed, thin and bright, and he turned his head to one side, yawning wide and pink and slow. 'Yes, indeed. And it's important you understand why I did it.'

'You killed the orchard?'

The cat sighed, arching his tail high over his back and down again. 'You see? I did *not* do that. That's what you remembered. What's the point?' He sounded annoyed. 'It was all within the rules. What I told the star was true. And the apple-lord – between you and me, what kind of lord *sleeps* for hundreds of years at a time? – insulted me.'

'Where have you come from?' I said. My voice sounded high and panicked. A noise in my head was welling up, growing round, repeating over and over.

'Oh, fine,' said the cat, 'just ignore my defence, then. Fine. Where have I *come* from?' His purr had turned into something darker now; a growl, basic and primitive, more like an animal. He lowered his head and then looked up at me with narrowed, amused eyes. 'Where do *you* think I've come from?'

'You were in a book, about the orchard. Em told me . . .' I spoke quickly, jumbling the words together. The cat did the best it could to shush me.

'Puh-*lease*. It's all simple, really. I'm here because of *him*.'

'Eren,' I said. There was no hint of a question in my voice. From above me, a small laugh floated on the wind.

'Eren!' I hissed, worried that someone else would hear. 'Eren, what is this?'

'What are dreams, and waking, and stories, and imaginings?' asked the cat. 'They're all, very much, the same thing, seen from different angles in different lights. Now, boy. Sleep. Sleep and do not wake until the light has returned. I'll go and take care of the star-boy again . . .'

Something deeper than fear made me move back inside, made me reach up and pull down the window, and even as I tried to look back again, to call to the cat – or to call out at all – my head was on the pillow. The air felt dense, heavy, crushing me onto the bed. I had no choice, I knew. I slept, a dead dreamless nothing.

⚏

'Look, I'm on your side! You know that!' Uncle Rob's voice was loud, strained.

I wasn't *trying* to eavesdrop, but they hadn't realised I was outside the door. I stopped, curious, and listened.

'Oli's a bright kid, Judy.'

I pressed myself closer.

'What is this about, Rob?' My mum's voice was quiet and polite. That was never good.

'I'm just not sure if you should keep him in the dark like this.'

'I appreciate that we all have our own views, and of course

120

I'm more grateful than I can say that you're letting us stay here, but—'

'*Listen* to me. I wonder if he doesn't already know. You must have noticed how ill he's been looking lately. He's pale, he's distant. What if he found some newspaper, or saw something on the TV at one of his friend's places?'

'Is this a rebellion, Rob? Is that it? You'd all rather make things easier for yourselves and ignore me and everything I'm trying to do . . . !' Her voice had got louder and higher and from the sounds in the kitchen Rob had rushed over to hug her. He made soothing noises, like he was rocking a baby to sleep.

'Judy, this will work out.'

'And what if it doesn't?' asked my mum in a tiny, cracking voice. 'What will I tell Oli then about his dad? That he's a traitor? That he's being denounced in Parliament? That the papers would love nothing more than to see us in rags, on the street? He's innocent!'

My dad? I pressed my ear close to the door, moving my feet slowly on the carpet, trying not to breathe.

'You think I considered him guilty for even a second? For heaven's sake,' Rob's voice grew louder again, 'I might not agree with James's politics, but he's no criminal. I never thought that. The thing is, someone, somewhere, is responsible for thousands of lives ruined, millions of pounds just . . . just gone from the pensions. They want someone to blame. James is caught up, but he will be freed in the end.'

'But what if he's not?'

'He will,' said Uncle Rob. 'You'll see. Listen to your brother, for once. We won't say anything to Oli, if that's what you want. At least you finally came here. That's one good thing already.'

'Never could with James,' said Mum in a small voice. 'I don't think he ever forgave you the protests.'

'We were young and proud. George, too.'

'George thinks he did it, though, doesn't he?'

Rob sighed. I heard something scrape against the floor – a chair being pulled out to sit on. 'George doesn't want to see you or Oli put through this hell. But George doesn't matter, in the end. Only the truth. James will come home.'

Mum's voice was almost a whisper. I held my breath to listen. 'Oli adores his father. I couldn't cope with him hearing such horrible things. Did you read what that nasty little woman said? The lawyer, the one with the cheap blue suit. Said that he had stolen from the very heart of the country itself! She said that.'

'I heard,' said Rob.

'How can she say that? How can that be allowed?'

'It's an accusation,' said Rob. 'Not a fact.'

'They're making him a monster, Rob. They're making him into a monster. I can't – I can't—'

'Shh, Judy. We won't say anything to Oli. Not me or Bekah, not George, not anyone.'

I backed away from the door, my mind numb, and moved silently back upstairs. Counting five minutes, I came bounding down the stairs, noisy as I could be, calling out to Jasper as I saw him, and stroking his belly as he flopped onto his side. 'Good dog!' I said, making my voice sound happy. 'Yeah, yeah, you are!'

'Oli! Morning!' said Uncle Rob, appearing from behind the kitchen door. 'Come on, lad. Have some toast.'

I let him ruffle my hair as I went past, and went to give Mum a hug.

FIFTEEN

Eren grins at me, leers at me, and then, like a clucking hen, pushes his chest out. 'Haven't felt this good in many a year, my boy.'

'I don't understand.'

'Course you don't. I'd call you a liar if you said you did! Anyway, what is there to understand?'

Everything is hazy. Nothing seems important. Where's Eren gone? I've lost him. I turn my head around, looking for him, calling out his . . . he's standing right in front of me, eyes flashing like steel blades in the dark.

'Hey up,' he says.

'I'm caught in a web. You're the spider. This is wrong.'

He looks bored, almost, and picks at his teeth with a long, sharp finger. 'Aye, well, there's nothing doing being all complainy. You can't really do much more now.'

He's right, I know – more than I've known anything else. Pain is bad, food is good, and I am here, and Eren is right. I try to cry, to kneel down and hide my head, but I just stare at him.

'Tell me,' he says, in a high, put-on voice, like a man

acting as a king, 'what stories are.'

'They're just . . . no, they're not *just* anything, are they? They're everything.'

'Oh, yes, you're very good. What is the end of a story?'

I manage a dry laugh. 'A beginning?' I ask. I've started to understand his games, at least. He's singing to himself, over in the corner, a song I can hear but a song not for me.

'A tale I know, de dum, de dum, I know of many a tale! To catch a boy, a cunning ploy, and one that never does fail!'

I wonder how long I've been here. I really, really don't know.

⁂

I MET UP with Em with the idea in my head. She was wearing a green straw hat, faded and crooked, and she beamed when she saw me and jumped down from the wall. 'Hey, stranger!'

'Morning.'

'Busy days, eh?'

'Yeah. How was that apple pie?'

'Tasty! You should come to mine and try some . . .' She looked down, awkward for just a moment. 'But maybe when my dad's not around. He . . . doesn't like the smell,' she lied. I scuffed the heel of my shoe on the pavement. I knew her dad wasn't a big fan of mine. He probably didn't think much of me, either.

'Listen, Em, is there, like, a library around here?'

She looked at me and scratched her chin. 'Uh, yeah, sure.

125

Local library? How come?'

'I want to find some stuff. About stories.'

'I could lend you some books I have. I just finished this one about a secret group of—'

'No,' I cut her off. 'No, not *a* story. More like . . . them all. How they work. What makes them.'

'Ri-i-ght,' she said, uncertain. 'Well, we can go to the library down by the council house. It's not great from the outside, but it's fine inside. I've been loads. We had a school trip when I was younger, and you had to find out about your own road using the histories and stuff.'

'Can you show me?' I asked, and she smiled and nodded. We caught a bus into the centre of town, a place I'd never been before, and all the while Em chatted and joked about nothing and everything. The clouds overhead turned darker, people around us got on, got off, read papers, chatted, sat and stared out of the windows at the passing world. It was good, I thought. It was *normal*, like a distant memory of a life I'd had. It made me think more of London, of getting the bus to school, being around my mates, being dumb and free and happy. Em kept prattling on and I laughed at her stupid jokes, not because I found them funny but because I wanted her to know how glad I was that this was normal, that this was safe. We got off at one end of a bustling high street. Em shot a dark look at the sky. 'Going to rain,' she said. 'Ah well! Come on, it's this building here.'

She pushed open a glass door built into an older stone frame. 'They did it all up new last year,' she said. 'Actually, I preferred the older library. It had cool corners to crouch in and books that never ever moved. They made it lighter, more fancy and electronic, but it's not as nice as the old one.'

'Shame.'

'Maybe. But now there's a wheelchair ramp. Swings and roundabouts, eh? 'Mazing.'

Behind the reception desk, with a smart, white computer screen pointing up at her, an older lady was typing, grey-streaked hair pulled back into a bun, a huge, soft-looking cardigan pulled high up to her neck. She smiled at us and looked back down at whatever she was writing. 'So,' said Em, letting the word trail off. 'Where shall we start?'

I walked over to the librarian. Why be shy? I figured. 'Excuse me.'

'Yes, dear?'

'I was wondering . . . I'm doing some research on stories. Like, the ideas behind them, what they mean to people. I wondered, do you know any books about that? Like, writing, maybe. About telling stories.'

She looked at me with expressionless eyes for just a few seconds, searching for something. Her gaze flicked up to Em. 'Nothing more specific, dear?'

'You mean, like, quotes from authors?' said Em.

'Maybe. Their thoughts about stories,' I said. 'Story*telling*.'

'Ah!' said the librarian, her gentle smile returning. 'I can do that – that's my domain! Here, follow me, I actually have just the thing . . .'

She shuffled out from behind the desk and called us over to

a bright paper display propped up against a wall. **WRITERS ON WRITING**, it said in cut-out sugar paper, with black-and-white photocopies of old, grizzly men, young smiling women, and all sorts of other faces stuck on around it.

'Here, have a read,' she said, pointing to a piece of text typed in deep black letters.

The universe is made of stories, not of atoms
Muriel Rukeyser

The librarian sighed happily and pointed to another.

To be a person is to have a story to tell
Isak Dinesen

'They're collected from all around,' she said, 'and I can point you to a few of the books themselves, if you'd like. Ah, how about this one? "The truth is in the tale. The world is in the words."' She read in a soft, distant voice that made me think, somehow, of rain falling on a garden.

'Beautiful,' said Em quietly. We were alone in the library, the three of us, but we were talking as if there were others to disturb. Ghosts, perhaps, I thought.

'Yes,' said the librarian, 'wonderful sentiments, aren't they? So many people write books just so they can understand the things that happen in real life.'

'And it works?' I asked.

She looked down at me curiously. 'It's not quite so simple, I think. The world turns, and there are new horrors and terrors every day. But it's like . . . like there is something deeper, something truer, going on. And if we can just tell the right story, we might all work it out. Poets and writers have tried for thousands of years to capture in words that spark of humanity that makes us what we are.'

Em pointed to another of the printouts.

The shortest distance between a human being and Truth is a story
Anthony de Mello

'Is that what you mean?'

'Hmm,' said the librarian. 'I suppose it is. But what did you want to know, specifically?' she asked me. I thought hard, staring at the display in front of me.

'What does it mean, all this?' I asked.

'I'm afraid I don't quite follow . . .' said the librarian.

I sighed, feeling them both watching me. 'I have a friend,' I said, 'who likes stories, a lot. I think he needs them more than anything else. And I wanted to find out what that meant – to only want stories, nothing more.'

'Ah, a bookworm!' said the librarian, moving slightly away, keeping an eye on the desk and the entrance. 'Oh yes, oh yes – there's always another story to explore!'

'What friend?' asked Em. 'Back home?'

'Yeah.'

'You tell your friend from me,' said the librarian, 'that there's no need to worry about the books running out. As long as there's people, there's tales. Always has been, and touch wood, always will be!'

She walked back to her desk to sort through some papers, the sound of her flat shoes slapping on the floor. 'You're a weird one,' said Em. 'What friend is this, who *needs* stories? Sounds barmy to me.'

'Maybe it's like an addiction,' I said. 'Some people need attention, don't they? Some people drink. Maybe it could be like that, for a good story.'

Em sucked at her lip.

Raindrops started hitting the windows high above us, slowly filling the room with noise. Em clicked her tongue and asked if she should call her dad to pick us up. 'Sure,' I said, 'we can wait here, right?'

'Payphone's just over there, I'll be right back.' Left alone, I looked up at the surly faces of the writers again, reading their thoughts and one-liners, and tried to understand. What was Eren doing? What did he want me to know?

※

The ride back home was awkward and strange. Em's dad didn't seem to like me, Em didn't want to talk, and we all sat silently as he drove. At my house, he stopped near the kerb. The rain was still falling, grey and dull, and I pushed open the car door ready to run for the porch.

'Thanks,' I said. 'For this.'

'Yeah,' said Em. She smiled. Her dad was staring ahead, both hands gripping the wheel.

'Thanks, again' I said.

He craned his head round to look at me and nodded, just once. 'Sure,' he said.

Em shook her head and glared at him. 'Bye,' she whispered. I shut the door and stood back, letting the car pull away.

❊

I went in, dripping, kicked off my shoes and climbed the stairs. Nobody else was home. I wondered, briefly, where Mum was. 'Eren!' I called before I was even in my room. He could hear everything in the house, even if he wouldn't leave that attic. 'Eren!' I shouted. I was angry and my voice came in deep, short bursts. In the air around me something shivered, like heat haze, or falling dust. I yanked at the ladder and didn't care when it crashed down noisily, hitting the floor with a bang. A tiny, distant chuckle sounded in the chimney. 'Eren, now!' I shouted again, and climbed up. He stood close to the hatch, staring down at me with a calm, fixed smile.

'You'd be better watching your manners,' he said, simply. I was panting slightly as I stood up and looked into his eyes.

'That cat,' I said.

'Yes?'

'What was . . . how did you . . . ?'

'Your friend Em told a lovely tale. It's a truth that's been twisted to magic. The best kind.'

'You can *do* stuff like that?'

'Make the cat real? Is that what you think happened?'

I hesitated, trying to understand. Everything he said sounded too certain, too complete. He smiled at me, then grinned, and sat down, patting the floor.

'I wanted to show you a wonder. Didn't you enjoy it?'

'What does that mean?'

'He was for you alone, boy. A gift, from me. Wasn't it nice? Fun? A talking cat! How many others could know what that's like?'

'What do you *want*?' I asked, exhausted. I sat down next to him, the rustle of his wings making my skin shiver. 'I should tell Mum and Uncle Rob, I should—'

'No,' he said. I nodded. He was right.

'You *could* do one thing for me, however.'

'What?' I asked, almost in tears. Something was wrong, I knew; something was terrible, but it itched in my mind without ever becoming a solid thought. Everything Eren said seemed too important to miss.

'That book of local stories. The one your *friends* were blabbing about. I want it.'

'Go and get it, then.'

'Manners, Oli,' he growled, so low the air seemed to move as he did. I nodded again. 'Why would I go and get it myself, when you could go and get it for me?'

A tiny half-thought tugged at my mind, but Eren leaned over and pressed one finger to my temple. 'Do it for me, eh?'

'I just want to know what you are,' I said in a whisper. He looked at me with pity and patience, a teacher struggling with a slow student.

'Quite right, too,' he said, and twitched his head towards

132

the ladder. I stood up to leave when he stopped me with an outstretched arm.

'I'm growing, you know. First the dreams, then the whispers, then the sights and the sounds. Oh, the things I can do when I'm strong, child! You'll get to see such wonders.'

'Are you *real?*' I said. My mouth was dry. Eren raised his eyebrows and laughed.

'Think you're mad, do you? You made me up? I don't think so. Here,' he said, moving forwards, 'how much *proof* do you want?'

He raised one talon, its sharp point glinting in the thin light, and he pulled it across my cheek. I cried out, backing away, a cold-hot pain bursting up where he'd touched me.

'*Real* enough for you?' he growled. He spat on the floor, shook himself.

'Kids,' he said. He turned his back on me.

'That hurt!' I said, holding my cheek. I could feel a thin line of blood.

'Truth hurts, don't it?' shouted Eren. 'Am I real, indeed? Boy, I am older than everything you could *dream* of! I am the very essence of stories and you and all your human world are nothing but *mist*, nothing but *vapour*, as far as I'm concerned!'

I clenched my jaw, my fist. 'You say that,' I said in a quiet, steady voice. 'But you need me, don't you? You keep on needing me, and the others, to tell you stories!'

Eren turned, very slowly, and his eyes flashed a dangerous red. Something made me step back again. The hair stood up on my neck. I was facing something truly, truly bad. I made myself breathe slowly and stared right back.

'I'm right, aren't I?' I said. 'You do need me.'

'You,' said Eren, 'are so interesting.'

'You what?'

He cocked his head. 'You're so special, Oli. So different. Maybe it's truth that I need you! But did you think that I *waited* for you?'

I stood my ground, watching his eyes, his feet, his shuffling wings.

'There's darkness and power in you, child,' he said, 'that call to me like blood in the night. You think you're the only one in this world? Pah! I could hear stories every day for a thousand years if I *wished* it. Your friend, Emma! Isn't *she* fine? Doesn't she know such *lovely* things? But you're better, Oli. You have something rarer. You've got heart. You've got darkness.'

My cheek stung. I touched my fingers to it.

'Don't ever doubt me,' said Eren. 'Don't ever think you can wish me away by pretending I'm not real.'

'What's wrong with Em's stories?' I said.

Eren shook his head. 'Nothing! Stories are good. Nothing wrong with her, either. Maybe that's the problem. Maybe it's the things that are wrong that I need. You have that, boy. That magic. That truth. Now,' he said, 'enough prattle. Enough breath. Tell me a true thing. Tell me a story. Your choice – but tell me something good.'

I blinked, tried to argue, opened my mouth, but something stopped me. If that was what he wanted, I'd show him. I'd show him how good I could be.

'There . . . there was a girl,' I said, 'who was searching for a baker. Every day she rode around, trying to find this one man, 'cause she had heard that he knew a secret. He was a baker for money, but a magician for power, and people said that he had found a way of contacting faeries. The girl only knew two things – that the man was a baker, and that he was her father. It had taken her all her life just to find out that much, but now she was hunting for him, just to know his name, just to see him. One by one she worked her way through all the bakers in a town, and then she moved on. The town she came to next, she thought, might be the one, so she'd never stop until she found him. One day, she was in a new town, to find the next baker on her list. The air in the bakery smelled like it always did – nothing special to her well-accustomed nose. Though the other customers were drooling, the girl had been in a hundred shops before that one, and she was immune, by now, to the temptations of fresh bread or perfect pastries.'

'This,' said Eren, 'is not something I ever worry about. You people have weird ideas of hunger.'

'The girl went to the counter, and asked to meet the master baker. It was always quite easy to get just a quick word, using her pretty looks, or a sad story – or even a lie, if she had to. Finding her dad made it seem OK to bend the rules a bit. In this bakery, the girl asked just to talk to him, and like in so many other places, the staff said it shouldn't be a problem – he was always happy when he baked, and a pretty girl could only improve that. Sure, they said, just through this door, but don't disturb him too much! Lunch orders had to be made. The girl went in to the kitchen, where a man was busy kneading bread. He wore a big white hat, with flour all over his chest, the usual. The girl decided to be blunt. "Excuse me," she said. He turned around and smiled, waiting to hear what she had to say. "I'm looking for a man who knows the faeries. Is it you?"'

'Direct, indeed,' said Eren, but he lay back and kept listening. He seemed to enjoy it. I smiled.

'The man's face turned into a frown. "I'll have none of that monkey business in here, please," he said. "If you're selling potions, be off. It's an honest business, here."

'The girl nodded and apologised, and turned around to leave. The baker frowned again and opened his oven to pull out the rolls. The girl froze, stopped dead in her tracks, and stared at him. "What is that *smell*?" she asked. "It's *amazing*. Like heaven, like every perfect meal I remember as a child, like liquid gold. I've been in every bakery north of this place, and never . . . never . . . it's out of this world! It's . . ."

'She stopped. When she had said those last words, the baker's face had turned sour and dark. "Go on," he said, holding a large rolling pin in his hands, and he looked at the girl very strangely.

'"You . . . you cook bread beyond anything this side of dreams . . ." she said. "That bread has been cooked with spices from beyond our world. You *are* him who speaks to faeries. You're the magician."'

Eren was watching me with a cold, animal hunger. If he had

licked his chops I wouldn't have been surprised. As I stopped talking, he only raised his head, just slightly, like an old man being roused from a nap. 'That's not the end,' he said, no question in his voice, just a distant, icy certainty.

'I can tell you the rest later,' I said.

'Oh? Hmm? What's that? Are you out of ideas?'

'I don't *want* to tell you any more now. I'm going downstairs.'

There was a cold, vicious fury in his words as he spoke next, something ancient and terrible and deathly. 'Maybe I will tell *you* a story, child, about the boy who played with fire, and then tried to run away. I could tell you how he burned.'

'Please—'

'Go, then. But come back. And I want that book, too, the book from that society. Bring it, hmm?'

His face seemed to warp then, pulsing and distorting until he looked almost, just barely, like a cat, purple-black fur and sly slits of eyes.

'Let's see how thin the curtains are, shall we?' he said, with a lick.

Oily smoke again, thick and heavy, and then nothing. I was alone in the loft, my whole chest beating, thu-thump, thu-thump, as my heart raced and raced.

SIXTEEN

'It's all so good,' says Eren.

'Hmm?' I feel so dazed. I can't tell if I'm sleeping, if I'm dozing off, if I was ever paying attention. Only when Eren wants me listening, I think. That's the only time I'm wide awake.

'It's all so good,' he says again. 'You've got a knack. A skill. You're a natural! Well . . . you're getting there, with my help.'

'Thanks,' I mutter. A stupid, thick-lipped thing to say. I'm not thankful. I don't feel anything. 'A dullness,' I say, out loud.

'Yes,' he says slowly. 'It's to be expected. Now! Let's just check. Do you know what a lie is?'

Oh, this again. It doesn't ever bore him.

'A lie is something that hasn't happened.'

'And when did it not happen?'

'Just the once.'

'And what,' he says, dark voice, dark eyes, dark shadow in my mind, 'is a story?'

'Oh, it's everything,' I say, exhausted. I could cry, if I had that much strength.

'Go on, go on.'

'They're the truths that didn't have time to happen,' I say. His eyes are wide amber moons in the dusk.

'You might have got it . . . !' he says, and there's actually a note of awe in his voice. He's impressed. 'You might have actually got it. Which means, of course, that I am truly winning.'

I smile, then forget why I'm smiling, so I stop. On and on and on. The moon passes across the sky.

⁂

I WANTED TO tell someone. Anyone. Mum, Uncle Rob, Bekah, or Em, or Takeru. But I couldn't. I hadn't thought about this, it wasn't something I had worked out was true, like a maths problem or an essay or a riddle. It was something deep and obvious and natural, that I could never tell anyone about Eren, that I could never give a reason not to sleep in the house, in that room . . .

That night I dreamed again, dreams of a lime-green forest. The trees were tall, silver bark pulled tight across the trunks and ripping like clothes that are too small. The leaves were small and sharp, pointed little streaks of pale green, mint green, and all other greens, making up the sky. The air was yellow with the power of those branches. I walked along a path, or what might have been a path, or the idea of a path. Bracken, brown and coiling, crunched, and something moved underneath. Somewhere behind me laughter rang out. I span around. Nobody was there. I heard it again, high, musical, hard to place. Leaves as bright as tropical frogs danced on a breeze

139

as I searched. Where was it coming from? Somewhere just beyond. Just a little further . . .

'A hiding place
You'll never find,
Just stare ahead
And turn behind!'

A tiny, singsong voice spun through the air. A kid? I tried following the noise but nothing made sense. The towering trees were silver and grey.

'Follow your nose
To find your bread!
Stay on your toes
To keep your head!'

'Who are you?' I shouted out, and my voice echoed like a dull, forgotten bell.

'We run and sweep and jump to bite!
We sing and dance and kill and fight!'

'Where are you? Cowards!' I called. In that moment, something changed. I hadn't realised the woods had been noisy, but suddenly, and completely, everything was silent. Had there been so much noise before? I didn't know, but now there was none, and my own breathing rang in my head like a rattle, every cracked twig became loud to me as a gunshot.

'You should beware insults, didn't I say?' said the cat, licking its paw absent-mindedly. 'There are places where they mean a lot more.'

'You!' There was a name I should remember. Something,

someone . . . something like a bat . . .

'Be careful, in the low places, not to insult those you can't see,' he said, and turned away, flicking his tail, and was gone. In the silence, a rustle of bracken echoed over and over. I jerked awake with a dry gasp.

'Who's there?' I said.

I was in my bedroom. The room was a deep, late-night blue and I rubbed at my eyes to focus.

A faerie tapped on the window.

'Spices from beyond the world!' he said. 'Prices from beyond the grave!'

'Eren,' I said, looking up, looking out at the stars, then at the faerie. He was playing games again.

'Will ye no' buy some?'

'What?'

'Warm those buns, baffle those loaves. Buy my fruits, eh, eh?'

'What do you want?'

'There's no telling,' said the faerie, his voice dropping into a growl. 'Who knows how I end up? Mebbe I just start lashing out.'

'I don't—'

'How's it end, eh?'

'What? End? I—' I stopped, suddenly understanding. Was he serious? Now? I could barely focus enough to talk. How could I finish a story with no ending?

'Give us a hint, eh?'

'Fine, fine, just . . . wait, OK? Wait.'

I took a breath. I opened the window. The night air stung

my lungs.

'The faeries had given the baker their spice on one condition: he had to swear that the spice would never touch his children's blood. Well, he thought he didn't have any children, so he agreed without a second thought. But now, everything changes. He panics. He can't risk his secret being discovered: no one can know he is a magician, he thinks. He has only one choice: to save his secret, he has to kill his own daughter – dead. So he does. A single drop of her blood falls and lands right in the bread dough, a red splash in the white bowl. He loses everything – his spice, his magic, and his daughter. The end.'

The faerie did some sort of jig on the branch, hopping from one foot to the other like an impatient, eager kid. 'That's it?' it said, raising a thin eyebrow. 'Aw!'

'Let me sleep,' I said. 'The story is over.'

It stopped its dance and leaned forwards, both hands resting on its legs. 'Just beginning!' it sang, high and joking, and then with a rustle of leaves and a whirl of dust it was gone, blinked away into air and empty space. I heard Eren's voice in the creak of the trees.

'I'll get the book!' I hissed and rolled over, shutting my eyes tightly and waiting for sleep.

⁓⧓⁓

Bekah brought me breakfast in bed. She hadn't woken me up since that very first morning. 'Rise and shine, chuck!' she said. I sniffed, cleared my throat and sat up groggily. 'Oli, you look sick,' she said, her face suddenly more serious. 'You feeling

OK? What happened to your cheek?'

She made to move her hand to my face.

'I'm fine, don't worry. Tired.'

She frowned. 'Not much sleep?'

'Last few nights,' I said. 'Lots to think about.'

She bit her lip slightly and put the tray down. 'Your dad,' was all she said. I looked down, then back to her. She was glancing at the open door, listening for Mum.

'It's not that, really. That's not what I meant.'

'Oh,' she said, trying to smile naturally again, then stopping, catching herself. 'You're too old to patronise, Oli. You're not dumb. You're a good kid not to push your mum, but you know something's up and you're not even *asking* . . .'

Not now, I thought. *Not Dad*. It was easier not to think about it. She passed me some toast and a cup of juice and took a triangle slice for herself, chewing small pieces, cupping her hand to catch crumbs. She ate like a mouse, I thought, in tiny bites and dainty nibbles. I ate my slice in four bites. I hadn't even realised I was so hungry.

'You should talk to your mum, Oli. Sometimes adults are scared as well and we all just want a hug as much as you might. Talk to your mum?'

'Did he do something bad?'

For a moment her face was blank as she looked at me, then around the room. 'No,' she said, 'he didn't, but some people are saying that he did. There's a lot of money missing, and the government's involved, and it's all got a bit . . . confusing.'

'Missing? From where?'

'You know the government looks after money that certain people save up for when they retire. Soldiers, doctors, loads of others. Well, they found out that a lot of that money's gone. It's been stolen.'

'Dad's not a thief,' I said.

Bekah nodded. 'No, honey, of course he isn't. But a lot of people are angry. When money goes away, people notice. And somehow your dad got caught up in it all. He had to stay – to clear things up with the police, with everyone.' She sighed and looked at the door again.

'I'm not a kid,' I said. I could feel Eren shifting in the loft, nodding, smiling, watching.

'You're not, really, are you?' said Bekah. 'So, talk to your mum, eh? But go easy on her. She's trying to protect you. It's complicated, but it's because she loves you. She doesn't want you to be worried, you see? It's coming from a good place.'

'OK,' I said. 'Sure.'

'Good,' she said, nodding and finishing her toast. She licked the butter from her fingers. 'You know your dad and Rob had some spat years ago and they never see each other now, but we are so glad you're here. You could visit more. Maybe we'll come down to London when this is – when – timings work out.'

'What spat?'

'Ancient history,' said Bekah. 'Your dad was doing a different kind of job then. He organised a new project nearby, some sort of building work, but there was a chemical plant involved. A few people got upset and thought it would ruin the area, pollute the environment. There was a campaign, and protests.

Rob and Em's dad, George, headed the whole thing up. They did a good job, you know. The project failed. I think it cost your dad a lot. He never forgave them, really. It all seems so stupid now, doesn't it?' said Bekah. 'What's past is past. We have to stick together. OK?'

'Sure,' I said. I ate more toast.

'Now that you're awake, a boy called round – Takeru? He wanted to know if you'll be coming out later.'

'Takeru? He's here?'

'He was, sleepyhead. It's past ten. I told him you'd call back.'

'Thanks, Bekah. Really. Thank you.'

'Sure. Any time. You'll be all right, Oli,' she said, and walked out of the room.

Shaking the crumbs from my sheets, and trying to do the same with all the thoughts in my head, I got up and dressed. With just one last look up at the loft door, I went downstairs.

SEVENTEEN

'The emotions you felt then,' says Eren. 'They were . . .
complex.'

'Emotions are complex things,' I say, surprising myself.
They don't sound like my words.

'Hmm. Yes. It's like a good meal. All things mixed
together, for a sophisticated taste. You get bored of plain
things, after a while, eh, smidge?'

I feel less and less like I want to answer. Less and less
like I can.

'A question!' he announces. 'A riddle! How do you know
a story is over?'

Over? Over? How could I know that? I run through all
the stories I know in my mind, flicking through from tale to
tale, looking for the clue. Eren's eyes burn.

'Happily ever after,' I say, but he waits for more. What
more does he want?

'A story ends,' I'm saying, 'when everything has happened.'

'Hmm. And how would you know when that is?'

The blackness around us is like smoke. It wafts lazily to
its own beat.

'Tick tock,' says Eren. 'Tick tock.'

'*M*AN,' SAID Takeru. 'That's *heavy*!'

'Yup.'

'I mean . . . wow,' he said

'I'm not sure how big a story this is,' I said. 'I think Mrs Barson knew.'

'It must be pretty big. This is cool!'

'Doesn't feel very cool,' I said quietly. Takeru looked at me and started to apologise.

'Don't worry,' I said. 'It's just . . . weird.'

'We could find out more,' he said.

'No,' I said, as firmly and as certainly as I could. 'No, I don't want to. I don't care what people think. I want to know what's real. I'm sick of stories and lies. I don't want to read what *might* be happening, what *might* be lies. Don't tell me, OK? If you hear things. OK?'

He looked serious as he nodded, just once, and offered his hand. 'Deal. And if you need help, just yell.'

'I'll make my way through the Portal,' I said. 'Seems as good a place to hide as any. Behind a bush by a fence. It's good, that. No troubles . . .'

We were both sitting on a wall overlooking a small, grubby playground. The swings were old and the paint was peeling off the metal, the roundabout looked too stiff to move, the seesaw sat sadly in the concrete. A minute, maybe two, passed before Takeru said, 'Heavy stuff, man.'

'Pretty much.'

He sucked in his breath and shivered, just slightly, in the pale sun.

'So your mum hasn't actually told you?'

'Bekah did,' I said. 'I think she felt bad about it.'

'Think your mum will?'

I looked away, looked up at the sky, squinted as the sun flashed out. Mum wasn't going to tell me. She thought that she could make it all not be true if she just pretended it wasn't. I sniffed and spat on the ground.

'My dad,' said Takeru, 'he's not around much either.'

'I haven't seen your dad yet,' I said. He shrugged.

'Yeah. He and Mum have kind of been fighting for a long time. He's always at work. He stays away for days. And Mum pretends it's all a big party when he's away, like we can do whatever we want. But then she goes out and the house is empty – well, apart from me.'

He stared down at the ground. I picked at my nails.

'Sorry,' I said.

'No biggie,' he said. The swings squeaked when they rocked in the breeze.

'Sorry your dad's in trouble,' said Takeru.

'Yeah.'

'I wouldn't worry about Em's dad,' he said. 'He's always in a mood. When I was younger I broke one of their windows with a tennis ball. You have no idea how scared I was! I thought he'd go mental. His face got all red and he started shouting even before the ball had stopped moving. I called him The Volcano until Em gave me a bar of chocolate to make me stop.'

I laughed. 'The Volcano! That's good. Quiet, normal, but any moment—'

'He could erupt!'

We jumped off the wall, laughing, feeling lighter.

'It might be time to bring it back,' I said.

'I can't. I've been bribed,' said Takeru. 'Chocolate, remember? But you're free still. Volcano's all yours. And if Em gets to you, I'd name a higher price.'

'Sure thing. I'll strike a mean bargain, and split my rewards with you,' I said.

'Sweet.'

'Yeah.'

We quietened down, wandered the playground, kicked at the dirt.

'We should do something,' said Takeru. 'Take your mind off it all.'

'Anything,' I said.

'Come on,' he said. 'We can head to mine. You any good at shoot 'em ups?'

'I'm all right.'

'I need someone to beat. Em's too easy. She doesn't really get it. Says the stories don't make sense and then she gets shot in the head and sulks.'

'Stories,' I said, spitting the word out. 'Last thing I need.'

'What you *need*,' said Takeru, 'is to *stay alive in the face of imminent alien invasion*. Come on.'

We headed back to his house. The driveway was empty, the lights turned off. 'See?' he muttered. 'Out.'

Inside he offered me a drink and we headed up to his room. It had a good view of the garden below, and through the trees

I could see Em's house, and the roof of Uncle Rob's. The loft window was black and still. I looked away. Takeru noticed.

'Yeah, I see Em coming a lot,' he said, flicking on a TV and choosing a game from a bookshelf. 'We built that door years ago. We used her dad's tools, did it in the evenings, after school, on Sundays. We felt like spies. We were so scared our parents would find out and go mental, but they never cottoned on.'

'It's cool, though,' I said.

'Saves a bit of time,' he said. 'Now, red or blue?'

'Uh, blue,' I said. I'd never played the game he'd chosen, but the goal seemed pretty basic; alien invasion of earth, and only us left to save mankind. The aliens – growling, many-legged monsters – made a very satisfying splat when you shot them. It was clear pretty quickly that Takeru was winning.

'Aim for the eyes,' he said. 'But the big grey ones – there, like that – you have to take the legs out, and they have these babies – no, that's a mine! Yeah, that's right, sidestep – who run faster so you have to use the machine gun with the laser or they suck your health.'

'I need a bazooka!' I said. Takeru nodded.

'That,' he said, 'we can do.'

We spent the next few hours saving the world from various threats, while eating pretty much all of Takeru's parents' supply of crisps and chocolate-covered raisins. I felt right again. I felt almost normal. Takeru opened the window to let some air in, asked me if I wanted a Coke, went to find some ice. I paused the game – I wasn't about to win, but I'd managed to nuke two entire planets, which has to count for something – and lay back, leaning against the foot of his bed. He had posters on his wall, of mountains, a desert, a dark, blue ocean. He came back in, two glasses packed with ice.

'Where is that?' I asked, pointing to the mountain. He looked up, smiled.

'K2,' he said. 'Second highest mountain on earth. Cool, right? It's the most dangerous mountain there is. More difficult to climb than Everest.'

I pushed myself up and took a glass. 'K2. You into that kind of thing?'

'I don't know,' he said, looking down. 'Maybe. It would be cool. Think about it – the most difficult mountain in the world. There's, like, three hundred people who have ever made it. It would be something special.'

'Adventure,' I said.

He nodded. 'Yeah. Get away from Coxborough. You know?'

'If you want to see London,' I said, 'when I'm back, I mean, I could show you. You could come and stay.'

His face lit up. 'Really?'

'Sure,' I said. 'I mean, we don't have any mountains—'

'That would be awesome,' he said. He lifted his glass. 'Adventure!' he said. I drank my Coke.

Half an hour later, Takeru had saved the universe. I'd died – eaten by some sort of space worm – just before the end.

'Don't worry,' he said. 'That bit's always hard. What do you fancy now?'

The wind moved the curtains. A bird cried out. Something rumbled in my mind, images of trees and fiery red hair.

Something smelled like spices and bread, and an old, sour smell of apples rotting in a field.

'I . . . I want to go back to the society,' I said slowly, picking my words one by one. 'You up for it? We should go back. I want to go and look around that room again.'

Takeru looked at me with a puzzled face, holding my stare for the smallest of moments, then chuckled once. 'Sure thing. Remember where it is?'

'I don't really know this place yet.'

'Hmm,' he said. 'I think I can find it. Shall we call Em?'

Did I want to call Em? It would be more distracting to have three people – more convincing for us to go together, but then, another pair of eyes to watch me – to catch me out. Takeru seemed to decide without me. 'Yeah, we'd better. It'd be a bit weird to go, otherwise.'

'Sure,' I said. 'But . . . best not mention about my dad. You know. The Volcano and all . . .'

'Got you,' he said. 'Come on, let's get Em and go and see the crazy lady. I mean, that's kind of the same thing anyway.'

He laughed at his own joke. I smiled. We made our way downstairs, and he locked the house back up. The driveway was still empty, his parents busy somewhere else.

⊰¦⊱

'You want to go back? Really?'

Em was standing in her doorway, one arm still hidden behind the front door. She turned to me with her hands moving to her hips, as if we were somehow insulting her.

'Seriously,' I said. 'I want to see more. But it'd be better with you. We don't know her, still.'

'Mrs Barson.'

'Yeah,' I said, 'Mrs Barson. You coming?'

She hesitated for a second more, looking closely at us, trying to figure out if we were playing some joke on her. 'OK,' she said slowly, 'just a sec.'

The door closed again and we waited, listening to the noises from inside, some muffled words, a couple of knocks. 'What a way to spend a lovely day,' said Takeru, shoving his hands into his pockets and walking back out to the pavement.

I followed him. 'Sorry if this is boring,' I said.

'Nah, please. What else was I going to do?'

Em's door opened again and she stepped out, bright pink-and-yellow hat pulled tight on her head. She looked pleased.

'Wow,' said Takeru, staring. 'It's quite a look you've got there.'

'It's summer!' said Em with a smile. 'We off to the society or what, then?'

She raised one hand to her head in a mock salute and started walking off. 'Adventures!' called out Takeru, charging after her. I tried to clear my head. *Get the book. I need the book. I have to get the book. For him.* The curtain in Em's front window twitched and her dad's face appeared, looking out. Our eyes met. He flinched, then tried to smile. I hurried off after Takeru, determined not to look back. *Let him think what he wants.*

We walked lazily, slowly, making jokes and stopping whenever we wanted. I tried to push all my worries, all the truths I was learning, deep down inside of me. I wondered what Em really knew.

'Oh! Hello, again,' said Mrs Barson as she smiled down at us and pulled at the front of her cardigan.

'Uh, hi,' muttered Takeru. 'We're – well, Oli thought—'

'I really enjoyed your stories the other day,' I said. 'I actually wondered if I could see that book again. With the myths.'

For a moment she didn't respond. Then, with an enthusiastic nod, she stood back to let us in. 'My, we could have new members in the making here, eh?' she giggled, and we walked through to the library. 'Was there a particular tale you'd like to find?'

'Well, I guess, all of them,' I said.

'Hmm,' said Mrs Barson, peering at me over her glasses. 'Do you think you're likely to be here long, dear?'

'Oh, sorry. If you're busy . . .'

She held up her hands. 'I apologise. I meant here in town, with your mother. But really, I shouldn't pry.'

Behind her, Takeru spun his finger in a circle next to his ear. *Crazy*. Em kicked his shin, and he winced silently, hopping.

'Well,' she continued. 'Here's the book.'

'Thanks,' I said, taking it from her, feeling its weight in my hands. It seemed so small. I thumbed through the pages while Mrs Barson watched. Takeru sat down by the window, his eyes tracing around the room. There wasn't going to be any way to steal the book, I realised.

'It's all so weird,' I said. 'So weird and cool.' Em cocked her head and looked at me with a smile. Mrs Barson nodded slowly.

'Do – do you think I could *borrow* this?' I said. I felt Takeru watching me, saw Mrs Barson's confused face turn softer, saw

Em raise her eyebrows slightly.

'Oh,' said Mrs Barson. 'Oh, I'm not sure. We don't usually—'

'Please,' I said. 'It's just really interesting. And, you know, I'd like to know more about the area. I might be here for a while . . . because of my dad . . .'

I trailed off and waited for my words to have their desired effect. She sighed and shook her head with a chuckle. 'Of course,' she said, 'of course. What use is a book that's never read? I'm sure you could use some fun distractions.'

'Um. Yeah,' I said. 'Yeah, totally.'

Takeru stared at me, then turned to Mrs Barson, and let his eyes roam upwards, to the owl skulls perched high above us. 'I could use some distractions,' I repeated.

'You're really into this, eh?'

'I guess.'

'You totally are!'

'And what's wrong with that?' asked Em. We were walking back home, and I had the book safe in my hands. My thumping heart was still drumming in my ears.

'She seems a bit bonkers,' said Takeru.

'She is not,' said Em, pushing past Takeru to move ahead again. He winked at me and cupped his hands to his mouth. 'Come *on*, Em. You know I'm joking. The book's cool. And Oli's *got* it! You never managed that, eh?'

'I didn't ever ask! I was happy just having that room to explore.'

'Calm down! It's not a competition.'

'I've been going there for ages without *you*, Takeru.'

'Guys, don't fight,' I said. 'Come on, it's not that big a deal.'

'Maybe not for *him*,' said Em, pointing a finger at Takeru, who took a step back and raised his hands.

'I didn't say anything!'

'You—' started Em, but she stopped suddenly, turning to the road. A car had pulled up level with us, the two men in the front turning our way, the window already sliding down.

'Hey, guys,' said the passenger, and touched his forehead with one finger in a tiny salute. He smiled, and looked at the three of us, from one to the other. The driver smiled too, hands resting on the wheel, his head craned forward to see.

'Uh,' said Takeru.

'*Keep walking*,' said Em, pulling at my sleeve and glaring at Takeru.

'Sorry to bother you kids,' said the passenger. 'Don't suppose any of you know a boy round here—'

The driver elbowed him in the ribs and shook his head. 'We're off,' he said. He nodded again towards us and pulled away, saying something as he did so. The passenger turned around and stared back at us. He looked at me, smiled, and wrote something down on his hand.

'Just lost, maybe,' said Takeru.

'Or creeps!' said Em. She turned to me, saw me clutching the book and put a hand on my shoulder. 'Or worse,' she said. 'Or nothing. Come on, let's go.'

We walked quickly back to Em's house, then to Takeru's, hardly saying a thing, stopping every time a car came round the corner, not knowing why we were all suddenly so edgy. I turned more than once to see Em looking at me like I was a puzzle to solve.

When I got home I ran upstairs and hid the book under my pillow, as if he wouldn't find it, then went downstairs and played the piano, making noise, making music, anything to drown out the buzz in my head. Mum walked in, her eyes red with tiredness.

'Maybe Rob could teach you,' she said, indicating the piano.

'Mm,' I said.

She stood in the doorway, tapping her fingers together.

'Were you out?' she said.

'Friends,' I said. 'I went to Takeru's place.'

'Oh, that's nice.'

I hit the keys, making jarring, noisy chords.

'Well,' she said. 'Well. Good.'

She turned to leave. I slammed the piano lid.

'Oli!' she said, her voice suddenly louder. 'Careful, now. That was your gran's!'

'Dad,' I said. 'Are people saying he's stolen something?'

Mum went very still. She rested one hand on the doorknob.

'Stolen?' she said. She gave a high, fake laugh. 'What? Of course not. What on earth made you think so? Why would you say that?'

I looked at her, my mouth open slightly. 'Right,' I said. 'Mistake. Never mind.'

'Well,' she said. 'OK then.'

You liar, I thought, and Eren thought it with me. Mum laughed again, smiled at me, shaking her head, and turned around and walked out. In the air, in the silence, I knew that Eren was talking. You see? he said, you see? They're all such liars!

⊰⊱

The next day was a Sunday. Clouds covered the sky, bland, doing nothing, not changing. Bekah was in the nothing room, humming to herself, reading a book. She looked up when I walked in, knocking gently on the door.

'You don't need to knock,' she said. 'Don't be daft.'

'Right,' I said. 'Sure.'

Jasper was sitting at Bekah's feet, his head resting on the floor. He perked up when he saw me, got to his feet, trotted over. I leaned down, scratched his ear, thumped his side.

'He likes you,' said Bekah. 'Eh?'

'That makes one,' I said.

'Oh, don't be like that. Nothing less attractive than a self-pitying man. Anyway, you seem to have made friends.'

I shrugged. It was true, I guess. Jasper walked away, walked back, jumped up at my knees.

'Good boy!' I said. His tongue lolled from the side of his mouth.

'Oli,' said Bekah. 'What I said before . . .'

I looked up.

'I don't want to stick my nose in where it's not needed, but I just thought I'd say, you've been so patient with your mum. You have. It's good of you.'

'Sure,' I said, but I wanted to ask more. Jasper was still walking around me, wagging his tail, jumping up.

158

'Oi,' I said. 'Stop it.'

'Wants a walk,' said Bekah. 'Ah, the price of affection, eh?'

I leaned down and patted his head. 'You want a walk?' I said. 'Walk?'

Jasper barked, danced around, looked at me. 'Ha! He knows that word!' I said.

'Honour bound now, you are,' said Bekah. 'You can't tease him. He won't forgive you.' She coughed. 'Your mum,' she said, 'has been feeling very conflicted.'

I didn't look at her. I rubbed Jasper's ears, smelled his weird, outdoors scent.

'Sometimes she wants to pour it all out, and then she thinks that she's protecting you by keeping it all in. She wants you to be happy more than anything. I think it's killing her, a little bit, that there's this thing between you, now.'

'I told you. I'm not a kid,' I said, staring at Jasper's fur.

'That's as may be,' said Bekah, which didn't mean anything. 'You're her son, though,' she added, 'and that means so much to her. She's so proud of you. Keeps telling us so.'

Silence for a beat, for two, for three. 'Oh,' I said.

Jasper barked and jumped.

'Want a walk?' I said again, leaning towards him, not looking at Bekah. He barked, rushed forward, then rushed out of the room, bounding down the corridor, searching for something. He raced without looking, and with a sudden skid ran straight into—

'Ow!' shouted Rob. There was a thump, then a crash of something breaking. I looked at Bekah. Her mouth was open in surprise.

'Rob!' she called. 'What on earth—?'

Uncle Rob came round the corner into the room, the front of his shirt dark with something wet, and a broken mug handle in his fist.

'Damn dog!' he said. 'Raced right into me. There's tea everywhere, and my mug – just *look* at my— Bekah, why are you *laughing*?'

Bekah was looking at Rob, her hands raised to her face, her shoulders shaking as she tried to hide her laughter. I smiled, started to snigger, looked back at Rob.

'You're not serious,' he said, still frowning. 'My shirt!'

As soon as he said that, Bekah lost it. She was laughing so hard that the book she'd been reading slipped off her lap and landed on the floor. She looked up, wiping her eyes.

'Oh, I'm sorry, love,' she said. She took a breath. 'Ahem. Sorry. You looked *so* angry, I just . . .'

And she started again, doubling over as Rob scowled. I tried to hide my face, turned away from him, towards Bekah. She caught my eye and we both laughed even harder.

'Bloody dog,' said Rob, and he stomped out of the room.

'Oh!' said Bekah, wiping her face, clutching her sides. 'Oh, we have to stop! Oh, but . . .'

She kept laughing, holding up one hand to me. 'No! No, it's too funny!'

'Bloody dog!' I said, stomping my feet, doing an impression of Rob.

160

'Ha!'

'My best shirt! Bah!'

'Oh, you've got him to a tee!'

She took another deep breath. I looked at the door, looked back, smiled at Bekah.

'Good old Jasper,' she said. 'Good old thing.'

On cue, Jasper appeared again, an old, red leash in his mouth. Bekah and I burst into more mad laughter.

⊰⊱

I spent the day walking, reading old books, putting things off. I went round to Takeru's, not stopping for Em, not using the secret gate. When I got to the door I heard shouting, something bang, and my hand froze at the knocker. I backed away again, up out of the driveway, hoping he wouldn't see me. His parents' shouts rang out in the cold air and something – a glass, I guessed – smashed inside.

⊰⊱

Night came, and I couldn't wait any more. I took the book to Eren. He was standing in the corner of the loft, hands clasped together, eyes closed, half asleep, half praying, waiting.

'Ask and I shall receive,' he said. His voice made the hairs on my arm stand up. I smiled.

'I brought it, like you wanted.'

'Clever boy, you.'

'You want me to read for you, or . . . ?'

'Just put it down, there's a lad,' he said. I threw the book to

161

the floor, where it skidded in the dust and lay in front of him.
He sniffed. 'Wherever did you learn manners, speckle? Books
should be shown more respect than that.'

'Eren,' I said, but stopped. His eyes were keen and wide.
He scuttled towards me and I shivered.

'Oh, say it again,' he asked.

'Eren.'

'Yes?'

'I . . . I want to know more. Where did you come from?'

'Aha!' he laughed, and danced on the spot from one foot
to the other, a strange, weightless jig. 'What is Eren, what am
Eren? Oh yes, oh yes indeed, tee-hee-hee!' In a rush of wind he
stood behind me and whispered into my ear, his hand clasped
over my mouth to stifle my shout. 'Wants to see more?'

He let go, stumbling back to the book, picked it up and
started leafing through the pages. I stepped towards him again.

'Yes!' I said. The book slammed shut with a single, echoing
thud.

The world spun.

Everything stopped.

Everything started.

I was standing on a cliff, a swirling, tangled jungle spread
out far below. Eren tapped my shoulder and pointed with one
claw. 'Down here,' he said, 'is something terrible.'

'Terrible? What?' I asked.

He shook his head, tutted, lowered his eyes and kicked at
the dirt. 'Death,' he said, quietly. 'Death of so many things.'

'Who died?' I peered down into the trees, but we were

too far away. In the air, insects droned, bird cries echoed and died, strange croaks and high screeches swam and bubbled.

'Come on,' he said, and the air shimmered. We were standing in amongst the trees, the warm, damp soil sinking beneath my feet, the tropical air hot and wet and sticky. Something tiny bit at my hand and I slapped it away.

'*Look*,' said Eren, his voice barely a whisper. He shuddered. 'I so rarely come here, any more,' he said. I followed his eyes and gasped. A man was lying on the ground, his chest rising and falling slowly, too slowly. He was naked, staring up at the sky, wide, blood shot eyes staring and scared. His fingers trembled as he grasped at the soil.

'What's wrong with him? We have to help!' I said, moving towards him.

'Please, child,' said Eren, loud as thunder. 'Don't you get it? He's been dead for longer than you can imagine.'

'Who is he, then?' I said, looking away, looking back. He looked pathetic.

'Oh, he's the last,' said Eren. 'The last of his people. All the others are gone, already. He thought he could run, but no. No. Got him too. A virus,' he explained, seeing my face. 'Wiped them all out. He'll be bones, and then less than that. And no one . . . *no one* . . . wrote anything down.'

And then I understood. I saw Eren's face, pained and angry, and watched the dead man as he lay dying in Eren's dreams. 'Stories . . .' I said. 'It's their stories that are dying.'

'He's the last!' said Eren, pointing at the man, moving forward and looking down at his face. The man didn't change, didn't blink, stared at the sky and waited to die. 'He is the only one who knows his entire world's worth of treasure. You know what he's thinking right now? You want to know?'

'Eren, I don't—'

'He's thinking that he's scared, and that he doesn't understand. *That's* what fills his head.'

'Please—'

'He has completely forgotten,' he continued, his voice filled with rage, 'everything else that he learned, that his *people* knew, and now, in a second, it will all . . . be . . . lost.'

The man gave a shudder, closed his eyes, and finally, his fingers grasping at the earth, stopped breathing.

'Death,' said Eren, and looked at me.

'Monster!' I said. We were back in the loft, the cries and heat and smell of the jungle already gone.

'They didn't die 'cause of me,' he said. 'But I mourn what I miss. We all do.'

'So that's what you are, then? Memories and whispers and selfishness.'

He looked at me silently. Outside, a fox screamed.

'You think that,' he said, 'but you come back, eh? You and me, lad. We've got a lot to give each other. You know what I like about you? You're really very interesting. You remember that, eh? Eren thinks you're interesting.'

I shivered. 'Am I really . . . special?' I asked.

'You are,' he said, holding his hands together like a saint, raising his head. 'And you have no idea what I could show you if you agreed, if you *stayed* here with me.'

'I could stay?' I said. The words felt wrong and dark, a secret I'd just dared to whisper.

'Yes!' Eren shouted, a tooth-filled grin splitting his face. 'Yes! You'd be so . . . so . . .' He stopped and sighed happily. 'Ah, but what times we could have.'

'If I stayed. Here. With you.'

'If you stayed here with me!'

'How . . . ?'

'Questions, questions!' said Eren, swatting the air in front of his face. 'No time for those things. Just time for stories and fun and games and hope and wanting things.' He looked down at me. 'What're your hopes, spotling? What're your wantings? Think about *that*. Mark *those* things, Oli, boy.'

We were quiet for a while, not looking at each other.

'You're special, y'know,' said Eren. I snorted and sniffed. 'No, no, you are,' he said. 'Your mind. Your heart. I don't play with just anyone, you know. Not just any. But you . . . you're my kind of boy.'

'I'm rubbish at these stories,' I said, almost sorry for it. He laughed with bright, wide eyes.

'Ha! No, oh, no, no, no you are *not*. Your friend, little Emma, she's good – could be great, one day, with the right little push – but you're better. A natural, all ready for the plucking. She's pure and light and . . . innocent. You have the fire. The *mark*. I see it. I know it. There's nothing *rubbish* about you, lad.'

'Hers are better. Her stories,' I said, more hesitantly this time. Eren shook his head.

165

'Nope. You have the sight to see the darkness in the tale, boy. You're one of the ones I can use. Yup, you're one of 'em. Really!'

'Are there others?' I asked. The things he said made me happier. I smiled at him for a second and he puffed out his chest. He shrugged.

'There have been. Some are special and some aren't. You get to see me, you lucky pup! I had another friend, y'know, years back, way back when. Right here. She's gone now, though. Too long ago. You know how it is.'

I didn't. 'What?'

'This same house, you know. Years ago. Hundreds. She saw me and knew me. She wrote in her diary and the stories danced and we played together and laughed in the moonlight. She's gone now.'

'Why?'

Eren laughed. 'Hundreds of years, Oli! She died, for sure. I stayed. Sometimes I meet people who are like you and are . . . are . . . *fun*.'

'What was she like?'

'No,' he said. 'No dwelling on the past. It pains me, my child. Ha! But you read some of her diary, little spud! She used to write for hours in her diary, telling stories and sharing secrets. It's how I got in, how I met her. You even read some of the pages when I huffed and puffed and blew them. You plucked them from the air . . . and then I knew – oh, boy! – I knew another player had arrived.'

'The pages in the street, that blew around the car?' It was crazy to think of it, but it made so much sense, and as he

166

nodded I just smiled again.

'Her diary. And it found you. A nice link, no? All very neat. I was pleased with that.'

'Tell me about her!'

'No,' he said, holding up his hand with such speed I stepped back, and knew, without question, he wouldn't say any more. 'The past is gone. It's *you* here now. Oh, yes. You and me, mouse. Good times, eh? You're the one who's here now. You tell the stories. Go on with you, now.'

Dust and silence filled the space between us. My mouth was dry, or too filled with old words. I nodded, spat, and climbed down the ladder.

EIGHTEEN

His eyes are close to mine. He's chuckling, I think. He's breathing in my ear.

'I can leave this place,' he says. 'In the end, time gets hold of everything. You know what an animal has to do, to get out of a trap? It has to wait. In the end, springs rust, bricks crumble, walls fall, and all you have to do, to escape any trap, is exist longer than it does.'

'I—'

'When I first met you,' he says, holding up an arm to stop me, 'you asked me why I didn't just leave this place. Why I didn't go and do things for myself.'

I'm nodding, but he doesn't seem to care.

'Well, we'll have our answers soon enough,' he says, and smiles. He leans back and lets me continue.

⊰⊱

THEY KNOCKED on the door while we were eating lunch. Mum was playing with her salad, moving the fork around the bowl and resting her head on her hand. Uncle Rob turned his head in surprise, and Bekah's eyes moved to his.

'That scratch,' said Mum in a distant voice, still leaning on her hand, 'when did that happen?'

She ignored the knocking. I looked at her, smiled. 'Just playing. With Takeru.'

'Oh.'

Three more knocks sounded. Bekah put down her tea.

'Wonder who that could be . . . ?' she muttered, then stopped as Rob stood up. I watched him, chewing on my bread. The room was tense suddenly, as if we were hiding from the world. Rob went to the hall, shutting the kitchen door behind him.

'Probably selling something,' said Bekah into the silence. I nodded. Mum scratched her fork against the bowl and fiddled with her hair.

Uncle Rob's voice, loud and angry, sounded from the porch.

'What on earth . . . ?' sighed Mum, but as she stood she froze, her eyes fixed suddenly on Bekah, shaking her head. Rob's voice was muffled but he was talking fast, almost shouting, and then the door was closed with a slam that shook the frame.

'Oli, stay here,' said Bekah and she ran to the corridor.

Pushing my chair back I followed her, then turned, went over to Mum, put my hands on her shoulders. 'You all right?' I asked.

She turned to face me, smiling weakly. 'Tough times, Oli,' she said. 'Tough times.'

The kitchen door opened again. Uncle Rob came back in, followed by Bekah. He was breathing hard.

'From the papers,' he said, quietly.

'I knew it!' said Mum. 'I bloody knew it. It was always going to happen.'

'Judy, please,' said Bekah. 'No need to worry – Rob sent them away, and they don't have the right to just—'

'Vultures,' said Uncle Rob.

'They'll just wait. They'll just – *damn* it. Sorry, Oli.'

'What's going on?' I said.

'You can *stay*,' said Rob. 'You've done nothing wrong; they can't harass you like this. I'll call my lawyer.'

'We've been stupid,' said Mum.

'What's going *on*?' I shouted, and my voice echoed on the tiles. They all looked at me in surprise. 'Why are there reporters here now? It's about Dad, isn't it? Come on, I'm not dumb. *Tell me!*'

Mum fell into her seat again and looked at me with an empty face. 'You don't need to worry,' she said. 'You don't need to know about it all.'

'You keep saying that but it isn't true!'

'I just—'

'You can't *pretend* any more! I don't need protecting!'

Mum had tears in her eyes. She sniffed. 'Your dad . . .' she began.

Uncle Rob raised a hand and put it on the table. 'Judy, perhaps right now isn't the best—'

'Shh, honey,' said Bekah, taking his hand in hers.

Mum fixed her gaze on mine, her voice just a whisper. 'Should I have told you right away?' she said. Her voice caught in her throat and she stopped for a second. Uncle Rob stared at her, barely moving, barely blinking. Bekah leaned against him.

'It's so complicated,' she said. 'So big. Reporters, yes. Asking about your dad. Wanting to know what we know.'

'Em's dad. A couple of others . . . they knew. All along they knew how bad this was. But you kept it a secret.'

'If they follow the news, and they saw us, they'd work it out,' said Mum. 'George, Emma's dad, he already knew. He and your dad have argued for years. George always hated your dad's success.'

Rob snorted and Bekah hushed him again.

'Your father's not coming here. We might not see him for some time. And now the papers have found us . . .'

Her voice trailed off. I looked at her. I didn't say anything.

'I'll phone my lawyer,' said Rob, again. 'They can't badger you and get away with it. I won't allow it.'

Mum nodded and picked up her fork again. She looked frail.

'You should have told me,' I said again. 'From the start.'

'Oli,' said Rob, 'this whole thing—'

'You're not my dad, Rob,' I said. 'You're not. Stop acting like you are!'

'Oli!' said Mum.

'You should have told me! You shouldn't have lied!'

Mum's eyes were watery, her voice all soft and strange. 'Maybe,' she said. Then, 'Yes. I shouldn't have lied.'

'Dad might need me,' I said.

Mum gave a strange, shuddering sigh.

'I know about it,' I spat. 'About the pensions. I know, even though you don't think I do. I'm not stupid! I worked it out.'

The kitchen was quiet. Rob coughed, opened his mouth, but said nothing. I glared at him. Bekah was fidgeting with her hair.

'You know?' said Mum. There was no fight in her suddenly, no passion, no anger. I glared at her, balling my fists. I wanted her to fight. I wanted her to shout back.

'You don't care if I know,' I said.

'They just – we just wanted to keep you safe,' said Bekah. I snorted.

'You don't even care whether I know or not,' I said.

'I thought it was for the best, for you, Oli,' said Mum.

'Right,' I said.

'Coming here,' said Mum. 'One last summer. One last good memory. To escape. To avoid it all. Can't you see?'

'You *lied*,' I said. 'To me. You lied!'

'Oli . . .' said Rob, but I turned away from him, to Mum, to nothing.

'I'm going out,' I said.

'Maybe you should stay,' said Bekah, 'and we can—'

'No!'

Before anyone could move I threw open the door and stormed out.

⊰⊱

My mind was hot, a swarm of buzzing, a pounding pressure. I ran down the street straight to Em's house, heard someone shout behind me, jumped the fence. There was someone in the road, calling my name. The apple trees were duller than the last time I'd seen them. In the corner of my eye the tail of a cat flickered and disappeared.

She was sitting reading in the kitchen, her back to me.

'Em!' I hissed, tapping on the glass with my knuckle. 'Em!'

She looked up, startled, then relaxed when she saw my face pushed against the window. She giggled, tutted, came to open the door. 'You coming in?' she asked.

'No, come out, come *on*,' I said, stepping back into the garden.

She raised an eyebrow. 'You OK?'

I sighed. 'I don't know. No. No. Maybe.'

'Wow,' she said, and went to fetch her shoes. I was alone in the trees, and the wind blew cold. I looked up, across, at the attic window. I nodded, smiled, like I was part of some big joke, and looked away again, at the grass.

'OK, mysterio,' said Em. 'What's up?'

'Can we go through the flap?'

'You would use the Portal?' she asked, gasping dramatically, clutching at her heart. 'Are you of pure heart? Do you seek knowledge . . . or revenge?'

'Em, come *on* . . . I seek knowledge, OK? You want to know about my heart?'

I grabbed her hand and pushed her palm onto my chest. My heart was racing, filling my world with drums and noise. She nodded.

'The Portal,' I said.

'The Portal.'

We pushed through the bushes, through the leaves and

branches, to the dark where the soil was still damp. The fence was green and dusty with moss, but the hinge was good, and the flap worked as perfectly as ever. 'Not bad, right?' asked Em. 'It'll work till the end of the world, you know.'

'I believe you,' I said. I did.

We hunkered low in Takeru's garden, moving quickly, sticking to the border. Em filled her pocket with three small stones. 'Three shots,' she said. 'All I need.'

'Thanks, Em. He'll be in, you think?'

She shrugged. 'Let's find out!'

She chucked the stones with a grin, bobbing her head slightly as they pinged off the glass above. We waited.

'Too hard,' said Em, 'and I'd break the window. But too soft and he won't hear. Got to be careful.'

'Why don't we just ring the doorbell?'

She sighed and touched her elbow to my ribs. 'Isn't this more fun? 'Mazing!'

The sound of a door being opened made us freeze, and we turned to look up the path towards the front of the house.

'You think you're being subtle,' said a voice, 'but seriously, come on . . .'

Em grinned wider. 'Tak!' she yelled as he came round the corner. He smiled at me, stuffed his hands in his pockets and looked up at the sky.

'Wow! I *totally* didn't see you coming up the garden.'

'Shut up,' said Em.

'I'm glad you're home,' I said.

He looked at Em, confused, and chuckled. 'Who knew I'd made such an impression. Y'all right, Oli?'

I sighed, kicking at the ground with my heel. 'I don't know,' I said.

'You're acting kind of weird. Even by your standards.'

I looked into their faces, saw their eyes, honest and friendly, felt their gaze on me, and the sun high above, shining and solid.

'My dad,' I said, and the way Em shuffled her feet told me enough. She knew. Takeru didn't say anything. I walked forward, the gravel on the path crunching under my feet.

'It's a massive mess,' I said. I didn't know what I wanted to say. I just wanted to talk. 'I think we're supposed to be hiding, kind of. Because of Dad. I don't know what you know, but it's bad. Some journalists came round, they've found out where we are.'

'The men in the car,' said Em, then stopped. We all looked at the ground.

'I might have to head away again. I don't know. It's all kind of weird.'

'My . . . my dad has said a bit,' said Em, in such a small voice it surprised me. 'I think he's angry at the government. He said your dad's been found out.'

Her voice died away again. In the trees, the leaves whispered and giggled as the wind raced through. Deep in my mind, I saw the darkness of Eren's eyes.

'What do the journalists want?' asked Takeru.

'I don't know.'

'You, probably,' said Em, nodding towards me. 'Lies. Words. Gossip and lies and songs.'

'Don't think they'll want songs, Em,' said Takeru. She stuck her tongue out at him.

'There once was a man,' she said, 'who collected words. He put them in a special glass jar he had, whenever he found one he liked very much.'

'You what?' said Takeru.

'A story,' I said, hushing him. 'Keep going.'

'Well,' she smiled, raising her eyebrows, 'he had a glass jar. And, if you were talking to him and you used a new, exciting word that he liked, he would scoop it up, put it in his jar, and carry it off. He was a collector, I guess. Like an oologist.'

'A what?'

'Collects eggs.'

'Like a campanologist,' said Takeru.

'Huh?'

'Collects *bells*,' he said, knowingly.

'Stop being smart,' said Em. 'This man collected words, all the new and bright words he heard. So he was a . . . a lexologist. The problem, though, was that if he took a new word from you, he locked it up so tight that no one else could use the word ever again – not even you, who'd shown it to him in the first place. He was obsessed – he wanted them all. At night his bedroom shone like the Milky Way, the jars on his shelves dancing and spinning with trapped, silvery, exotic, beautiful, fancy words. People complained to him, of

176

course, but they couldn't stop him. No one knew how his jars worked, see, and there aren't any laws *against* bottling up words – no one owns them, no one sells them. But people knew. He took the word "constellation" and trapped it in a jam jar. Astronomers didn't know what to do! He heard the word "peahen" and gobbled that one up too, and then all the visitors to the parks and zoos didn't know what to say when they saw one. He took "gobbled" too, actually. All by magic.'

She paused, looking at us in the half-light of the path. Takeru waited for her to keep going, a slight smile on his face. The wind ruffled my hair and I swear I felt Eren's claws on my cheeks. I pushed the thought away, listened to Em, watched her spin the web.

She's good, Eren said, a whisper in my ear. *You're better*.

'Well, one day a man came to his door,' said Em. 'He was young enough, but his clothes were old, and he had a beard that went well past his chin. The man greeted him with a great big smile and a bow. "I have an offer for you," he said.

'"And what might that be?" asked the word-hoarder. He was suspicious enough of visitors, who might want to steal his words back, but he could never pass up the chance to talk to someone new, and someone so obviously from far away. Imagine what words he might have . . .

'"I know of your collection, and I admire your work," said the man. "But I wonder, does it not sadden you not to possess the Greatest Word?"

'"The Greatest Word?" asked the man. He shook his head

and chuckled. "I've never heard of such a thing. What rubbish! I've no time for this . . ."

'"Then watch this," said the stranger, and he opened his mouth to speak—'

'Oliver Munroe?'

We all turned, surprised, towards the road. A man was looking down the side of the house, peering through the shadows. 'You guys know an Oliver Munroe? Just wondered if I could grab a quick word?'

'You leave him alone!' shouted Em, so loudly that Takeru jumped.

The man stepped backwards, looking around the street. 'All right, sorry kids,' he said, turning away. 'Made a mistake, that's all. Have a good day, now. Just a mistake.'

'Come on,' said Em. 'Back through the gardens.'

Takeru nodded and pushed me back down the path, into his garden and down the lawn. 'My parents aren't actually in right now,' he said. He shot me a look. 'No need for all the sneaking. Just make sure those guys don't see.'

I looked back, watching the road as Em and Tak disappeared into the bushes.

NINETEEN

'When you tell a story, you expose your weakest heart,'
Eren explains. I don't know if he's moving his lips. Maybe
his voice is in my head.

'You lower those defences. All writers do, all stories
mean that. Letting something out. To strike a chord with
others. You've been foolish,' he says. 'Good, but foolish.
You must realise soon enough, eh, boy.'

'Don't . . .' I start to say, but he waves a hand through
the air. He creaks and jerks as he moves towards me.
Does he look that much like a bat? More like a spider,
I realise. He's like a spider.

⊱⊰

'OLI, DON'T—'
'No!' I shouted, marching away. I was angry now,
angrier than ever. What did they know?

'Come on, Oli. Let's go to my house,' said Em, pushing past
Takeru to catch me.

'Yeah, because your dad'd be *so* pleased to see me,' I said.
That shut her up.

'Oh, Oli . . .'

'Yeah, we all know what he thinks about my dad. Not my biggest fan, is he?'

'Come on, you two,' said Takeru. 'Forget them all. This is *us*, it's going to be OK.'

I looked at him, saw his confusion. Why didn't either of them see the real danger?

'We don't know what will happen,' I said, quietly. I stared down at my feet, trying to imagine the worst, trying to pray for the best. Somewhere nearby a crow cawed, sharp and empty, a harsh, dying sound.

'Oli,' said a voice, a gust of wind. I looked around.

'You don't have to be angry at *us*,' Takeru was saying. I ignored him, my eyes searching slowly up and down the road. I knew what I'd heard.

'Oli,' said the voice again, a rustle of dry leaves.

'Come and rest,' he said. *'Away from the risk, away from the anger. Come and have some fun, boy.'*

The voice was like the sound of thunder, or rain. It was the sound of tyres squealing on the road.

'Oh, *no*,' said Em, pointing at an approaching car. 'Shall we call the police?'

'Run, Oli. Run!' said Eren, his voice the rushing of the wind.

I couldn't say no to everything he was.

I couldn't say no to what he could do.

I ran.

'Oli, wait . . . !' shouted Takeru, but I was already off, my breath fast, my arms pumping. I ran as fast as I ever had, as fast as I could and then faster, ignoring the roads and pavements,

181

running until my side hurt. I left the street behind, left the cars behind, and when I stopped, finally, I knew that no one had followed me. I fell to the ground, panting hard, clutching my side and hissing through my teeth. A cat, white and orange, crept near.

'All right for you,' I said, shooing it away. The sun was bright now, thin clouds rolling away. The whole sky stretched above me. I knew with no doubt, the way I knew pain was bad and food was good, that I had to make a choice. The wind flicked the leaves in the trees. Eren waited. Despite the light, the moon was faint in the sky, a whisper, a chalk-white shadow of the night. Eren was waiting. He was waiting for me. I heard a cat howl, a dog bark, a bee nearby buzz and fuss. I had to choose something.

'*Come on, lad,*' he said, with no real voice at all. Adults always *lied*, always hid things from me . . .

There was a man, watching me, a small, bouncing dog on a leash at his side. I stood up, unclenching my fists.

'You all right?' he called. I nodded. My head was full of *noise*.

'I'm fine,' I said. He frowned, squinting in the sun.

'Right. Good. Here, don't I know you?' he asked.

I shook my head, my heart racing.

'I've seen you, I'm sure of it. From the school, perhaps? I do assembly there, sometimes.'

'I live here,' I said. 'In Coxborough.'

In the silence Eren screamed and sighed.

'No,' said the man, pulling his dog closer. 'No, that's not it . . . but . . .'

'What?' I said, louder, wary. The dog yapped and bounced.

'You're that guy's son off the news!'

'Shut up!' I screamed, as loud as I could, my throat and lungs suddenly burning. 'You shut up about my dad!'

My face was raw with anger, my voice wild and howling and fierce. 'Leave it alone! Just stop! Stop!' I stood for a second, frozen in surprise, glared at the man, spat on the ground.

'I didn't—' he began, then stopped, looking worried, looking around. 'I just—'

'The lot of you,' I said. 'The lot of you, shut up. Shut up!'

I ran, I ran, I ran. In the air all around, and the roar in my head, Eren sang and whispered his words. The dog was barking, echoing off, far, far away.

My face was hot and my sides were sore. I was alone, still raging inside. My breathing was hard. I was walking to Gran's house, to Uncle Rob's house. I had to find out what I could do. Em and Tak were probably looking for me, or searching for those reporters. Maybe they were even asking Em's dad about it all. I didn't care, I really didn't. In the high, clear sky, flocks of starlings twisted and turned above the pines. What a joke. All this light, all this space, and suddenly it all seemed so empty. I was angry, almost impossibly angry, clenching my fists and gritting my teeth. I spat on the ground again. Lies and half-truths and stories. Stupid. I knew things *they* didn't know. I had Eren. He was a story those journalists would kill for. He'd kill them if they even dared to tell the world. I was sure that he could kill, if he wanted. I smiled at that, then my stomach felt cold and heavy and I stopped. 'Eren,' I said under my breath. It was magic, that word. Pure, mad, magic.

'Eren, Eren, Eren. What do I do?'

Of course he could hear me. How could he not? He was in my head. White eyes in the night. Black eyes in the day. A quiver in the shadows, a haunting in the woods. Flames in the sky, cracks in the moon. He was *real*, something so much bigger than . . . than this! I slapped my hands against a fence post, kicked at a dandelion and left it, broken and dead. He was real. This was the joke. I walked faster now, almost laughing. He would be laughing too, up in the loft, up in the hidden, hiding place.

Yes, he would.

⁂

I knew Mum would be looking for me. Maybe Rob had phoned the police. I had to be quiet, getting into the house. The back door was best, and it wasn't even locked. Easy. I took my trainers off, tiptoeing in my socks. Every noise was sharp and clear. The clock was ticking. The wind rattled a window somewhere. A siren in the town wafted in on the breeze. I heard Rob's voice. I heard Bekah in the living room. I had to get upstairs quickly in case they opened the door and saw me. The shining painted banister creaked if you leaned on it too hard, so I kept my hands away, creeping in, creeping up. I knew he was shifting around in the attic, scurrying and watching. The weight of the house above me pushed down on my mind. Rob's voice again, a sudden bitter laugh. News of Dad?

News of me? I rolled my eyes at the closed door and hurried up the stairs. I didn't want any more mess. I only wanted the truth.

TWENTY

'Tell the story to its end.'

Does he sound bored? I don't think so. But he doesn't sound so alive, right now. Maybe there's a way out of this, if I can think quickly enough, act quickly enough.

'No,' he's saying. I drag my mind back to him.

'No, no way out. I was just feeling a little sad, kiddo.'

'What are you sad about?'

He looks at me with eyes that have seen too much. 'What have I got to be sad about? That's what you're asking me?'

I stand perfectly still, waiting. As still as night. As still as death. As still as a timeless song.

'I have seen worlds grow and die, until their ashes don't even float on the wind of the highest mountains. I've loved the legends of men whose names are lost, loved people who aren't even memories. The trees you climb now will be the coal that heats the rooms in a thousand years that house the babies that grow to found the empires that will crumble to dust while I sit and watch. I've seen libraries burn, my boy. I've seen books crackle and split and crack to black earth and shadows.

186

I've waited and slept and ignored more history than you and your islanders will ever know happened. Don't tell me I can't have a moment of thought before the bite.'

I frown. Before the bite?

—※—

We stand, just watching each other. Dust dances and circles around in the pale, chalky light of a moon. His wings unfold from his shoulders with a creak. He's strong.

—※—

I PULLED THE ladder up after me. I'd never done that before, not once since I first climbed up, not once since everything changed. It rolled away flat, well used and smooth, and I pulled the hatch door closed. No easy way down, today. It made the room even gloomier, despite the window and the afternoon sun. Years of dust can hide the light just as well as a curtain. Eren had his head to one side, watching me with a still, fixed grin, his claws folded behind him and resting on those wings. 'What's wrong, little mop?'

The silence swam around us, thick, old, dusty. Eren rustled his wings, soft as velvet. In the cold, black room I was suddenly less sure, less rushed and angry.

'Everyone,' I said. His eyes were wider than before. Nothing moved. The noise of the world behind the window hummed. 'Truth and lies. Dad. And you! The stuff you've been doing. They *all* just—'

'Yes,' he said. Deep in the blackness something changed

about him. He leaned towards me, smiling, showing his pointed teeth, all fur and breath and fire.

'So,' he said.

'So.'

'What's to be done? I've been enjoying things, up till now.'

Downstairs I heard soft bumps. Mum packing.

'My dad,' I said, but he shushed me.

He picked a spider from his fur. 'You'll stay,' he said.

'What?'

'It's how it goes, little man. You'll stay.'

'What do you mean, I'll stay?'

'Eggs is eggs,' he said. 'Night is black. Pain is bad. Sleep is good. These are truths. Well, you say they are. You'll stay.'

He was spreading his wings out. They shuddered, dry bones cracking, the fur and skin brittle and patchy. I thought of a canvas stretched tight over a tent, stretched till it broke and snapped.

'Eren,' I said, feeling suddenly sorry for him.

'Alone?' he said, his wings still stretching, turning up and out.

'I've got to go,' I said. 'It's over. I think we're going to leave.'

He chuckled deep and low in his throat.

'Pay attention now,' he said. 'Mind your manners, mind your step, mind your language!' With one thin finger he reached out to touch my forehead.

I shook my head. 'No game,' I said.

'No?' he said. He nodded, his hand frozen an inch from my face. 'No more games. Yes. And your mama?'

'What about her?'

'Running off again? Running with her, are you? Going to hide from the world? Little rabbit!'

'You shut up,' I said, staring at him. My throat was tight. I was angry again. He grinned like a devil, moved away again, and I snapped.

'*Shut up!* You just sit here in your loft and act all wise and clever, but what do you know about me? You can laugh and giggle all you want and get in my head and dance away in my dreams, but you're just nothing. You're just a shadow of a dead world! That's what!'

'And what kind of world you got here, boy?'

'This is mine!' I shouted, pointing to the window. My voice was a roar. I was screaming at him. '*Real* things! All the stuff you don't have. You're just—'

'You can run away, can you? Back to a mum who keeps you blind from the truth. Your dad's gone, boy, he's gone and finished. Going to play with your friends? Good little child! You can tell stories in the mud and make your little apple pies and pretend you're not *terrified* of everything. You child!'

'You're a monster! You're the child!'

'Bah!' he snorted. 'Look in your heart. Look in my eyes. Let's see what it is you really feel. Tell me this. Do you really never want to dream with me again?'

I stopped, stumbled, tried to shake my head clear. 'What can I do?' I asked. 'Everything's wrong.'

'Fix it,' he said.

'How?'

'Give in. Be what you can be, boy! Admit the way things

189

are.' He was moving towards me again. 'Let me,' he said. 'Let me see the whole tale, the whole, amazing thing. Give it to me.'

We stared at each other as the world turned outside the window.

'If I choose you,' I said, 'if I say I'll stay with you . . .'

'Yes?'

'What's it mean?'

'It means forgetting, Oliver Munroe. It means forgetting your pains and your nicks and your nacks and all that. It means not *being* forgotten, ever, by me, or . . . those 'uns downstairs. It means get-backs and little revenges on all the boring never-listens who spoke and spoke and never . . . ever' – he let his breath fall out, hot and dry – '*listened*. To your tale. Your story. To the story of you! And it's a good one, too. A good, good story. And believe me, child, from the likes of me, that is a *compliment*. I glory in the history of legends and nightmares, boy. I ride the dust of words spoken throughout all that ever was. That's what I am, and that's what it means! Being above death and above right and above wrong and above time and . . . beyond those things. Stories are *life* and it's stories what I know.'

I looked into his face, saw his eyes, saw the stars behind them and thought about Dad, about Mum and Jasper and Takeru and Full Lot Jack and sleeping cats and falling stars. 'Be more than human,' he said. 'Be more!'

'Dad—' I said, but he cut me off.

'Liars,' he said, 'and bad 'uns. *Protecting* you. As if you were weak. *Hiding* things from you, as if you were stupid! You see, don't you? You see?'

And suddenly, silently, in my mind, in my heart, something clicked. I nodded. He was *right*.

'I always listened to you, Oli,' he said. 'Isn't that right? I *always* listened to what you said. Your words are magic to me.'

And he had, hadn't he? Always listened. Always watched. Always paid attention. He'd always cared and never lied. To stay with him and dance in the stars, to see the red-hot sun of years ago . . .

He looked at me and smiled, sharp teeth and a pink tongue.

'Give up,' he said, and he raised one claw. 'This is your chance for adventure! Think of the wonders and the magic I showed you.' He was leaning forward. His feet clicked on the floor.

I raised my hand and reached out.

TWENTY-ONE

I know Mum looked for me. I know she looked in the loft, searched around, peered through the dust, but I was already gone. I'd already left. I'm part of Eren's world now. She'd never have found me. Nothing but shadows, here. Nothing but silence. He probably grinned at her, hidden in the corner, old and mad. There was nothing to see. Mum closed the door and left.

I think that was the moment, really, when Eren knew he'd won.

Every time I tell this, I know I'm getting weaker. Eren doesn't care, of course. It's all the same to him.

'And so I heard your story,' he says. I nod, numbly, trying to remember how all this felt, but I know that I can't. I don't know where we are. Maybe it's not a real place. Maybe it's a myth-place. I'm trapped here.

'It's a good one, mind,' says Eren. 'Tales within tales! I'm full, me. I'm stuffed!'

He wafts a hand towards me. 'Once more, eh? Just one more time.'

'It makes you stronger. Bigger,' I say.

'Mmm.'

'And me, do I just get smaller, then?'

'Once more!'

He's sucking the life out of me. I'm grey, made of shadows, made of nothing but wind and darkness.

'Once more might be all I've got,' I say.

'Then make it a good one,' says Eren. 'Go out with a bang. I've other stories to find, you know. I've other lives to live.'

I pause, picking at the threads of my life, gathering them all together, and then I start again. 'The car was rocking all over. Mum looked sick, poor Mum . . .'

Eren laughs a hollow, rasping laugh and settles down, the cat who got the cream, the spider with his fly, the storyteller listening to his own, perfect work.

ACKNOWLEDGEMENTS

I WAS WARY about writing acknowledgements. It seemed – it still seems – a bit too grown-up and smug. But since I first started writing *Eren* I've been rather silly and promised far too many people I would put them in the book.

This seems like a good chance to do just that.

I dedicated this book to my grandma, who died a few months before it was published, but I still want to recognise and thank my very patient friends and family.

Mum and Dad taught me to read, to love stories, and to ask questions.

Becky and Sarah put up with me and became friends as well as sisters (and Sarah was, and always will be, *Eren*'s very first reader).

Ashley, my wife, is probably the best person I know, and the little things she did, as well as her impressively unfailing support, mean a lot more than I can say.

Molly, my agent, and Sarah, my editor, are very clever people to whom I will always feel indebted.

Everyone at Constable & Robinson works very hard and sometimes it's scary seeing quite how brilliant they can be.

I don't want to bore you, so I'll stop there. There'll always be more people to thank, but I'll leave that for another book.

There'll always be more books, you know. There'll always be more stories.

Turn over the page to read

ℬRIDGE,
An Eren Tale.

Discover more about Eren's world and
Simon P. Clark: www.erentales.com

'Tell the story to its end . . .'

BRIDGE
An Eren Tale

THE BRIDGE had always been there, but she'd never heard the voice before. It called to her, over and over, saying her name, whispering things.

'Who's there?' she said. She moved a little closer and turned her head. 'Stephen? Is that you?'

The voice was too soft to make out. The light was starting to fade. The sound of water carried on the breeze. She shook her head, turned away, and ran back to the house.

The kitchen was busy, all steaming pots and scullery maids.

'Is there someone under the bridge?' she asked.

'What's that?' said Cook. She wiped her hands, panting a little.

'The bridge. I thought—'

'Oh, don't you go messing with that,' said Cook. 'There's fae in the bridge. You leave them be.'

She took a pinch of salt and threw it over her shoulder.

'Fae?'

'Never you mind, girl. Out the way now, there's dinner to make.'

'But—'

'Watch the roast!' shouted Cook, and she turned away, her face getting redder.

Peters was in the hallway, polishing the banister. His shoes squeaked when he moved. He winked when he saw her.

'Little Miss,' he said.

'What's fae?' she asked.

'Hm? Come again?'

'Fae. Cook said they're in the bridge.'

'Ohh you mean the Little Folk. Faeries, that is. Just an old story. I wouldn't worry.'

'Faeries?'

'Oh, yes. The bridge is the boundary. I think.'

He turned back to his polishing, the tip of his tongue sticking out of his mouth.

'What do you mean, boundary? Boundary for what?'

'Oh, I don't know. Hunting rights, maybe?'

She crossed her arms. 'But what does *that* mean?'

Peters paused his polishing. He put his hands on his back, puffed his cheeks out. 'I'd ask your father. He'd know more.'

She rolled her eyes. '*Fine.*'

The door to the study was closed. She stopped to look out of the landing window. She could see the bridge and the trees behind it. The river was fat with snowmelt. It flowed higher than usual, lapping against the grass by the banks.

Lia, said the voice. She frowned, took a step closer to the glass.

Lia, it said. *Help me.*

'What are you?' she said. Her breath fogged the pane.

Help me, it said. *I'm in trouble.*

'How do you know my name?'

The world outside was silent. She touched the glass. It was cold.

'Hello?' she whispered.

From beneath the window came a raw screech, a flash of black and white, the sound of beating wings. A magpie burst from the bushes. Lia jumped back. The bird flew higher, the sun flashing on its tail, and then it was gone. The study door opened. Her father peered out.

'Darling!' he said, surprised. 'Is everything alright?'

She looked at him, unsure.

'Um,' she said.

'Yes?'

'I . . . I just had a question.'

He opened the door wider, inviting her in. 'What's that?' he said. They stepped into the study, its walls lined with books, the air thick with the smell of smoke, and something else, something sweet.

'It's about the bridge,' she said. Her father picked up his paper.

'Yes?'

'They were saying downstairs that there's fae in there. And that it's a boundary. I was wondering . . . ' Her voice trailed off. She felt silly and young.

He looked at her a moment, blank-faced. Then he smiled. 'Oh, *that*. Local legend. Gosh, that's an old story. Now, how does it go? Our family made a deal with the fae. We won't hunt beyond the bridge all the way up to the woods and in return they won't hunt on our land.'

'They hunt?'

'Well, of course.'

'For what?'

'For what? For babes! What did you *think* fae hunt? I don't think there's much else they want,' he said. 'Peskies, my father called them. *The peskies in the water.*'

'Peters called them the Little Folk?'

'That too, yes. There's a few names.'

For a moment they were both quiet. Lia cleared her throat. 'There's someone there,' she said. 'There's someone under the bridge. I heard them talking.'

'There shouldn't be.'

'But I heard them.'

'Peskies?' he said, raising an eyebrow.

'No. I don't know.'

'Hm. I'll call Rogers, have him take a look. Could be a vagrant.'

'*Could* it be the faeries?'

Her father laughed, took a sip of something honey-coloured. 'Now, now,' he said. He smiled. 'Anyway, they couldn't come this side, could they? The boundary, remember? So, nothing to worry about. I'll have Rogers take a look.'

'Okay. I guess . . .'

He nodded, rustled his paper, and turned to his desk. The conversation was over.

At breakfast the next morning her father called her over. 'We had a look around the grounds,' he said. 'Didn't see anyone.

5

Thought I'd let you know. Must have been one of the fellows working on the garden.'

'So there's no one?' she said.

'No one,' he said, and he squeezed her hand. 'Now, hurry on, you have lessons later.'

She chewed her toast, stared out the window. The sky was grey, getting darker. It was going to rain soon.

'I'm going to go outside for some air,' she said. 'While the weather's okay.'

'Hm?' said her father. 'Oh, fine, fine.' He was reading something. She went to find her coat.

It was cold. The wind was coming down the hills, bringing more frost with it. She stood on the bridge. The water ran higher and higher.

'Hello?' she whispered. She pulled her collar tight.

Lia, said the voice. *Lia. Will you help me?*

'Who are you?' she said.

No name. Many names. Too many, maybe. There was something like laughter in the air.

She swallowed. 'Are you . . . are you fae?'

The voice didn't reply for a while, and when it did, it was different. Playful, thought Lia, and whining.

Fae? it said.

'The . . . the faeries. You live in the bridge. If that's you, I mean. Are you?'

Faeries in the bridge, said the voice. It sighed and grew louder. *Faeries in the bridge? Yes. Yes. And what else?*

'Um,' she said. 'I don't— what do you mean?'

What do you know?

'That this is the boundary. You can't cross it,' she added, louder, raising her voice against the wind. 'You can't,' she said again, and then she stepped backwards.

Ohhhh, said the voice, so low it was almost a growl, like the rumble of a stomach. *Can't cross. Yes, yes. Fae. In the bridge. Can't cross. Yes.*

Somewhere under the bridge, where she couldn't see the water, something splashed.

Help me, said the voice. *Please. Please, do.*

'What's wrong?'

Help me.

'How?' She looked back at the house. Would her father be watching?

Please, come and help.

'I don't know how.'

Come and see, said the voice, *and tell about the fae.*

She heard another splash. She smelled something strange, like smoke and candles and dust and fur.

'I don't know,' she said.

I just want rest, it said. *I just want aid.* It sounded hurt, now, like an old, wounded thing.

'If we go to the kitchen, I can—'

Just come down. Please. Please, young Lia. Come and tell me about the fae. Come and tell me what you know.

'But—'

Tell me what you know, said the voice.

Lia's face was cold. She should call her father. She knew that.

She took a step closer to the water.

She should call Rogers, or Stephens, or Cook. If someone needed help, or food, no one would mind.

She took another step closer.

'Can . . . Will I see you?' she said.

Yes. Yes, of course!

More splashing, but further down, still out of view.

She was right up by the bridge now, so close she could reach out and touch the stones. They were frozen, rough, too hard to rest against.

One more step, said the voice, *and you can tell me about the fae.*

She looked back again. She felt the spray of the river as it poured over the rocks.

I just want to hear the story, said the voice.

'But—'

Just the story.

'I—'

Just the lovely words. You have them, don't you? I smell it. I hear it. Please, Lia. Why not?

She bit her lip. It sounded so sad. And faeries were nice, weren't they? What harm could they do? She'd read that they were nice, in the books she had in the nursery.

'Maybe,' she said. She bit her lip. 'But only for a second, right? And only if you if tell me your name.'

Yes, yes, I will. I agree.

'Okay,' said Lia. 'I'll come down.'

She took another step, right across the boundary, and walked into another world.